THE HEATHER IS WINDBLOWN

Eve's trusting heart was too easily deceived. Just as events seemed to be taking a brighter turn, her vivacious cousin, returned to blight her life. Could any man resist the sensuous beauty of Shelley Anne? But Eve wasn't interested in any man. Just one man — the mysterious Paul Smalley. Who, or what, was he running from? Should Eve listen to the warning voices in her head, or follow the instincts of her foolishly trusting heart?

ANNE SAUNDERS

THE HEATHER IS WINDBLOWN

Complete and Unabridged

LINFORD
Leicester

First published in Great Britain

First Linford Edition
published 1998

British Library CIP Data

Saunders, Anne
  The heather is windblown.—Large print ed.—
Linford romance library
1. Love stories
2. Large type books
I. Title
823.9'14 [F]

ISBN 0–7089–5357–3

Published by
F. A. Thorpe (Publishing) Ltd.
Anstey, Leicestershire
Set by Words & Graphics Ltd.
Anstey, Leicestershire
Printed and bound in Great Britain by
T. J. International Ltd., Padstow, Cornwall

This book is printed on acid-free paper

1

From the first light, a grey poltergeist of a wind had moaned through the churchyard, torturing the branches of trees into submission, rustling down the main street to rattle windows and have an uproarious game of toss with a paper bag and a discarded newspaper.

Head down against the buffeting, the ends of her scarf streaming out like a pennant, Eve was suddenly blinded by a shower of grit. She should have stood her ground while sight was restored, but the new headmaster was due that morning at the school where she taught her boisterous bunch of fifteen year olds. She was no later than usual, but she wanted to steal the time to comb her hair and generally put right the mischief of the day before the bell went for morning assembly.

Living on the wind's edge of a

moorland town, retiring Mr Yates was used to Eve blowing into the hall like a four minute mile scarecrow. New broom Mr Smalley, unseen as yet but already nicknamed Mr Big by the children, might take a less tolerant view.

So Eve just kept going. And so, also, did the character emerging from Laura Thymes bit-of-everything shop. The collision winded Eve more than the force eight that had already socked the stuffing out of her.

'Why don't you look where you're going!' was justifiable comment, because it was her fault.

Hands steadied on her shoulders, strong and right. The grit factor was limiting and Eve did her best to blink it out of her eyes. She didn't query a stranger's presence in Hawsbury because it was just catching on as a tourist attraction. She only felt sorry he'd come when the calendar had gone crazy and it was difficult to believe, even with England's changeable

2

climate, that officially it was Spring.

Answering his expressive eyebrows, which, as sure as the heather is windblown, in eye language were curling to ask, 'What's the hurry?' 'I'm late for school.' It never occurred to her to tell him she wasn't a pupil and that she taught in the school. 'It's Mr Big's first day and I can't afford to be late.'

'Mr Big?'

'The new Head. He'll find out soon enough that I don't possess a streak of brilliance, but I hoped to blind him to my other faults by being tidy and early. Only — flicking an agonised glance at her watch — 'I haven't a chance of being early, so at least on time.'

His head went back, accentuating the squareness of his jaw. She thought this indicated a firmness of character and a doggedness of purpose. Stubborn as a mule she would have said in assessing this same characteristic in one of her pupils. At the same time it came zinging at her that the peaty brown eyes were flamed with amusement, while laughter was licking up the corners of his mouth.

'Oh, yes! Anybody unfortunate to have the surname of Smalley, would be nicknamed Mr Big.'

Eve was on the point of asking him how he knew the new headmaster's name, thought of the amount of gossip that went on in Laura Thymes' shop from which he'd just emerged, and decided it was an irrelevant question.

She mused . . . to think today had started off as an unspectacular numeral on the calendar. Just like any other day she'd waved to her friend Avril, who had been arranging pottery in the window of her curio shop, and turned sharp left at the bottom of the hill to bring her in line with Laura Thymes' shop. But there, unlike any other day, things had taken a spectacular turn. Her mind sparkled to think there was something about today that would get itself remembered.

That was the good. The bad was

the disconcerting realisation that she was more than a little put out that this briskly stepping stranger by her side, because they'd fallen into step and had started walking automatically, should first see her all wind-ravaged.

As a child she had been toothbrush thin, with a bristle of rich copper hair. She could now look her mirror image in the brown and green-flecked eye. The stem had rounded and the hair had tamed into deep waves; its colour had ripened to a lush chestnut brown. Her most ardent wish had been to 'catch up' to Shelley Anne. Shelley Anne was Eve's cousin, the only child of her father's brother, Richard Masters and his wife, Dorothy. As children, standing side by side, one had resembled the utilitarian toothbrush, the other a trim stick of candyfloss. A spun-sugar, fragile featured girl doll. Pink and white, with the contradiction of flashing black diamond eyes and hair silkily dark and luxuriant.

It was whispered around that if

Dorothy Masters hadn't been a person of the highest morals, one might be forgiven for suspecting Shelley Anne of being a changeling.

Eve remembered climbing on to the arm of the leather chair to reach the big, leather-bound dictionary in the hanging bookcase. She had laboriously read. Changeling: a child substituted for another, especially one supposed to be left by the fairies. She thought it was a very beautiful idea. She had sat, denim legs crossed, eyes screwed tightly closed and 'seeing' dainty gossimer winged creatures linking arms to deliver Shelley Anne. She imagined Aunt Dorothy exclaiming joyously at the exquisite fairy child, crooning over the perfection of her and not caring a jot for the 'Eve' sort of child she'd been substituted for.

The child Eve had often wondered where the other cousin went. Did the fairies take her away, or did they hide her inside Shelley Anne and would she outgrow this envied delicacy and emerge a gawky schoolgirl? Her baser self hoped this was the case, and she looked forward to the day when Shelley Anne would be all painful angles and thin awkwardness. At the same time, Eve was aware this wasn't very nice of her and she worked at conquering this nasty streak in her nature.

Eve never actually wished for Shelley Anne to be spirited half way across the world, but it seemed like the answer to a prayer when Aunt Dorothy and Uncle Richard emigrated to Australia. It didn't work out, and so they came back. The hot Australian sun had scorched Aunt Dorothy's nose, but Shelley Anne looked as if she'd lived under a perpetual sunshade.

Perhaps it was rude of her to stare, she didn't know. But she stared all the harder when the unbelievable happened. Shelley Anne's tongue speared her tiny pink mouth. Not only did she pull her tongue out at Eve, but those beautiful flashing eyes crossed to her nose.

Eve had to clamp her mouth shut to stop her own tongue poking out. Had her cousin somehow divined her bad thoughts, and was that grotesque look her punishment. And then, even more unbelievable still, Shelley Anne's face dissolved into angelic tears.

When Eve's mother asked: 'What's matter my lamb?'

Shelley Anne replied: 'Evie stuck her tongue out at me and pulled a horrid face.'

'I didn't,' Eve had protested. 'I only thought it.'

She supposed thinking it was only a mite less dreadful than the deed, if anyone believed her. In the event, she received a most painful slap.

After a brief sojourn in England, Shelley Anne's parents decided to try their luck in South Africa, and once more Eve's little world regained its calm when the annoyance of Shelley Anne was removed.

South Africa hadn't worked out either, and since then neither had a few other places. At the moment, Aunt Dorothy and Uncle Richard were trying their hands at being restaurateurs in Spain. Shelley Anne was living and working in London. Eve hoped she would stay there. She hoped it wasn't omniscience that was bringing Shelley Anne so vividly to the forefront of her mind.

As she and this handsome stranger skirted the school railings, it came to Eve what an idiot she was in letting this golden opportunity slip through her fingers while she fritted away her thoughts.

Shelley Anne had been the girl to grab the goodies at long-ago parties. Eve, too shy to help herself, had waited for some kindly grown-up to spot her dilemma. She had long since realised that some things in life weren't going to be presented to her on a plate. But what do you do when you're falling apart gauche and you can't think of a thing to say as you swing through the black iron gates and drop down the two steps into the playground, except: 'Bye.'?

He shouted something after her, but the wind blew the words back in his face. Eve hoped it was something about seeing her again. A herd of elephants thumped their happy expectation in her chest, and she simply dare not look back because her face was a scarlet give-away. It wasn't becoming to her years to show such eagerness. Yet that thought slaughtered her with wry humour. Why she should bother about her years she didn't know, considering they'd done precious little for her! Even by pulling rank and cheating on heels, she was still shorter than the majority of the girls in the sixth form.

She belted into the staff room. Alice Meakin was inelegantly postured, elbows on the window sill, eyes hugging the playground. Being her senior, Eve always approached this lady with a certain caution.

'You haven't sighted him yet then?'

No prizes for guessing the identity

of the person Alice Meakin was on the look out for. The fact that she was still looking meant that he hadn't arrived yet. Praise heaven, there'd be time for a repair job, although — catching sight of her hair in the staff room mirror — a complete overall would be more in keeping.

The grey head swung round. Briefly, Alice Meakin was a tall, thin disciplinarian of the old school. She disapproved of everything about Eve, in particular her unorthodox approach to lessons and when Eve goofed, as inevitably anybody who sticks their neck out must, she trotted out the merits of the three R's. Frugal with her smiles at the best of times, she sniffed parsimoniously, and swept out without answering. So what had Eve said wrong now?

She didn't pursue this line, because hitting the wrong note with Alice Meakin was her speciality. Even at the beginning, when she had been a shy newcomer to the school and Alice Meakin's jealous carpings had

had a very real sting, some instinct had told Eve that the senior mistress was not necessarily mean by nature, but had been ill-used by life and this had sharpened her to a fine point of intolerance. A person's good opinion must be worked for. But even as she reasoned this out, it was sometimes difficult to conceal her hurt. She had done nothing to earn the obvious hostility. Avril Speight, the friend who owned the curio shop, had confirmed Eve's thoughts by hinting that Alice Meakin was so life-soured that anyone young and fresh and happy, would automatically be disapproved of.

Eve accepted that must be the case and had no wish to probe deeper into another's personal hurt. Which didn't prevent her from listening to snippets Avril knew of Alice Meakin's narrow and luckless life. Her world war two soldier sweetheart had been posted missing and presumed killed only weeks after they celebrated their engagement. Years after the war ended, she had still been hoping for the miracle of his return, and had devoted herself to caring for her ailing parents. Her father died three years ago; she still cared for her mother.

Oh well! On a gentle sigh, Eve slipped out of her coat. She was tugging a comb through her hair, which was proving totally inadequate to the task, when the door burst open. A brown head thrust itself round, and Eve found her jaw dropping as she stared into surprised-as-she-felt peaty brown eyes. It was her handsome stranger. The mystery man she'd bumped into outside Laura Thymes' shop and left at the school gates.

'I say, should you be here?' was the perplexing question he fired at her.

'Too right I shouldn't.' She should be maintaining quiet in the hall. But she had the feeling that wasn't quite what he meant. Eve experienced a sort of hollowed out knowledge, mixed with chagrin and fierce inadequacy. And she knew why Alice Meakin had gone prune-mouthed and mute. She hadn't answered her because she had watched Eve and the new Head approach the school together — and what must he have thought of her mad flight across the playground! — and Alice Meakin was miffed because Eve had spoken to him first.

Just to add to her horror, Eve could feel the sensation of bright, burning blood rushing to her cheeks.

'You . . . you're the . . . '

'That's right.' He dipped his head gravely. 'I'm Paul Smalley, the new Head. If you get out before you're caught, I won't snitch on you.'

Filing that to puzzle over later, Eve held out her hand. She had some idea she should welcome him. The thinness of her veneration acknowledged his youth and the humour still round his mouth. 'I hope you enjoy the school as much as the school is obviously going to enjoy you. I'm Eve Masters.'

Slowly he emerged from his stupor to say: 'Thank you, Eve. You must think

I'm a nut. It's only just beginning to dawn on me that you teach here?' He made it sound like a question.

'Of course.' Her hazel eyes sparkled bewilderment. 'What did you think?'

He rubbed the side of his nose; his mouth curved. 'I'll tell you sometime. Preferably in the congenial atmosphere of the Elephant and Castle. And not before I've mellowed you with your favourite tipple.'

She found herself grinning right back at him. Well, wouldn't you? If she persisted in skipping across the playground like a schoolgirl, could she blame him for mistaking her for one?

His mouth was making mischief again, so she wasn't a bit surprised to hear him say: 'In this funny old world, why shouldn't Eve Masters be the Miss, and Paul Smalley, Mr Big?'

'I . . . Oh!' Her fingers clapped against her mouth, stemming the exclamation. Her eyes were as round as tureens. 'I'm sorry for calling you Mr Big.'

'All right, don't look so anguished.' His dry tone was neutralised by the crinkles saucing up his smile. 'Having given me the name tag, you're surely not afraid my sense of humour won't match up?' He reached for her hand in a straight-forward, uncomplicated way, tucking her fingers into his in the matiest possible squeeze, as if to emphasise it was friendship, of the platonic nature, that was on offer. 'It'll be quelling enough to resist a laugh every time the children call me Mr Smalley. Do you think you could call me Paul?'

Only with immense difficulty. Just saying his name under her breath quickened her heartbeat. At the same time her inherent caution was hammering it home to her that she'd be well advised to take Paul Smalley in small sips. He might be young for a Head. What? Twenty-nine? Thirty at the most. It was still a maturer vintage than she was used to.

2

Paul was completely unlike his predecessor. Mr Yates had been kindly aloof, strict, fair, but not always easy to approach. Paul made it known from the start that he wanted to be treated as a colleague and an equal.

Inevitably, the time came when a discussion spilled beyond the school room into the warm and congenial atmosphere of the lounge bar of the Elephant and Castle.

'How long have you been here, Paul?' Eve asked. 'I mean at the school.'

The question startled him. He dealt in achievements, not time.

'Three weeks . . . a month . . . '

Just as work absorbed every particle of his mind, so Paul absorbed hers. Eve's parents good humouredly put up with the perpetual chant of, 'Paul says . . . ' Being a hospitable soul,

Clarissa Masters had intimated that Paul would be a welcome guest any time Eve cared to bring him home. Eve knew the invitation was unmotivated. It was the sort of warm, neighbourly gesture Clarissa Masters extended automatically, which made their house the open, friendly place it was.

Since his illness, her father hadn't been able to go out as much as he used to, and Eve knew he would welcome some intelligent male conversation.

She pushed her fingers through her hair; it bounced back into its crisp waves. 'I know it's overdue, but would you like to come for a meal tomorrow evening?'

'Why yes, that's very kind of you. Are you sure?'

'No need to check. Mother told me to ask you before. I know you're still lodging with Mrs Taylor and she's a dear soul, but . . . '

'She makes lamb taste like dry old cardboard,' he finished for her.

'Mother makes her own bread.' In her mind that typified domesticity. 'She got the urge when Dad had his stroke. Only a mild one, thank goodness, but she had to bash her fear out on something, and so she chose a batch of bread dough.'

'Is your father all right, now?'

'Yes, I'm pleased to say.'

'You know, when I first came to Hawsbury, I was under the impression you'd always lived here. But that's not true, is it?'

'No. We moved here about a year ago. For the slower pace for Dad.'

Hawsbury was fine for someone of her father's age, but — and this wasn't a new thought, but had been pressing for a hearing since she'd first clapped eyes on the new Head — why had Paul chosen to submerge his bright intelligence in this dull backwater? Hawsbury was a retreat, a place to return to when life had given you a beating. Or it could be a hide-out for someone who wanted to get lost. What had precipitated that thought? Why should Paul want to get lost? What could he be running away from?

'Do you mind!'

She swallowed. His discernment, the way he knew that bit more than he was told, was quite something. Then she realised that he hadn't said 'Do you mind!' in the sense of someone who feels his privacy is being invaded, but quite the opposite. He was the one who was delicately questioning.

'Mind what?' she said uneasily.

'Oh . . . this slower pace you were talking about. Swopping a big alive city for a small sleepy town, which I presume is what you did?'

'You must be psychic, because yes, that's it. And at first I minded terribly. But there was nothing I could do about it. I was all set to jet myself out of the nest when Dad's health let him down. He begged me to let it make no difference and go just the same. But my mother was in too much of a heap to cope alone. And so — ' Shrugging, she lowered her eyes — 'I settled for a teaching post at Grange Lane Comprehensive. And here I am.'

'And very glad I am. Oh, not of the circumstances that detained you, but glad you're here, Eve.'

His sincerity was a flattering indication of . . . tiptoeing into new ground. She felt excited and taut and scared. Numb-scared. She had no provocative tricks to staple this moment to this new beyond-friendship area. And yet, if she didn't do something, react in some way, Paul would think his overture was stymied by lack of interest, and not wiles. He would never believe that anybody could be so ill-equipped in the ploys of love as she was. Her tongue felt stiff in her mouth, and her head was so erect it might have been sitting on a poker.

Paul's eyes seamed with tiny laughter lines. 'You don't have to ice up on me, you know. I wasn't thinking of overstepping the mark. I promise to stay in the square you've chalked out for me, so now will you relax. You're quite safe with me.'

Yes, and she would continue to be safe if she didn't stop acting like a witless schoolgirl. There was neither joy nor justification in the way she was behaving.

'And now what's bothering you?' he said.

'If I could tell you that,' she said on a small laughing sigh, 'there would be no problem.'

The talk reverted to school matters for a while. Then with a customary glance at his watch, Paul said: 'Drink up. Time to take you home.'

At her door, Eve's closely curled fingers slackened to accept Paul's hand. A thought was clicking away quietly in her mind. If she hadn't iced up on him, as he'd called her retreat into gaucherie and shyness, he might have been kissing her, instead of shaking her by the hand.

'Don't forget you're coming for supper tomorrow.'

'I'm looking forward to it,' he said.

Next morning, Eve told her mother that Paul had accepted the invitation to supper.

Clarissa Masters said: 'Oh, that's splendid.' And was happily away planning a tempting menu. The post had come early that morning, before Eve got up. A letter had arrived, with a London postmark, that made absorbing reading. It wasn't until Eve had gone shooting half way down the street that Clarissa Masters remembered she hadn't told Eve about Shelley Anne's letter.

She didn't consciously delay the telling; it just so happened that it slipped her mind until the evening. They had eaten. Paul had praised her cooking and she thought what a nice young man he was, and now they were relaxing over coffee.

'There was a letter from Shelley Anne this morning. Shelley Anne is my husband's brother's child,' she explained for Paul's benefit. 'Her parents are living in Spain at the moment.

Shelley Anne shares a flat with another girl in London. Well, apparently, she's been involved in a car accident. Oh, she wasn't hurt. In fact she had a miraculous escape, but she would like to come to us until she feels less battered.'

Eve saw the interest and compassion kindling in Paul's eyes and knew a wearisome sort of bitterness. Just by mention of name, Shelley Anne evoked a kind of magic.

'Why can't she go to Aunt Dorothy and Uncle Richard in Spain? Why does she have to come here?'

Clarissa Masters drew a shocked breath, and sharply reproved her daughter. 'Eve, that is unworthy of you. Shelley Anne might prefer to go to Spain for all we know. She is coming here out of consideration to her parents' feelings. She doesn't want to worry them by telling them she's been involved in a car accident.'

Paul nodded, as if applauding that praiseworthy thought, and sent Eve a very puzzled look. Eve, feeling miserable, saw her release in the unwashed supper dishes. She was glad to slip into the kitchen and leave Paul talking to her father. Not one look had passed between father and daughter, but while she knew the others were seeing her in a very poor light, Eve felt that somehow William Masters understood and had ranged himself on her side.

Paul's disapproval walked with her all next day, and Eve was both surprised and delighted when he suggested calling for her about eightish for a stroll down to the Elephant and Castle.

He came ten minutes early, but she was ready and, after chatting briefly with her parents, they linked arms to walk down the street. Outside they were amiable friends, but inside they were uneasy strangers.

'You don't know,' Eve wanted to scream at Paul. 'You don't know what havoc Shelley Anne can cause in what you thought was a predictable future.'

She suppressed the urge to snatch Paul's hand up to her cheek and declare what her heart felt before Shelley Anne stole him away from her, and she could no longer even pretend to herself that one day he might be hers.

Eve secured a small corner table, while Paul went to the bar to order their drinks. He set a shandy in front of her. She didn't expect him to understand the jealousy twitching her into despair any more than she could explain it to him. It hurt to see the laughter in his eyes grow still.

Eve was making such a conscious effort to regain her composure and somehow get them back on the old familiar footing, that she wasn't even aware of twisting her glass round and round until Paul slapped her fingers and gently rebuked her for fidgeting. Just as if, she thought wryly, I was one of his pupils.

The teasing laughter was back in his glance, coupled with a look of tolerance that Eve found more irksome than his displeasure. 'Would you like to tell me about Shelley Anne?' he invited perceptively. 'It's a curious sensation to sit with a girl who's haunted by the ghost of another.'

Eve adopted what she hoped was a cloak of affability. 'She's the most beautiful girl I've ever seen.'

The cloak obviously had rents in it, because Paul shrugged his shoulders and quoted: 'I do not like thee, Doctor Fell. The reason why I cannot tell.'

Not the sort of thing most likely to appease. 'Perhaps,' Eve said testily.

The mood between them was so badly impaired that she thought it best to bring the evening to a speedy close. When he picked up her empty glass and said: 'Same again?' She replied: 'No more, tonight, thanks. I should go home. I've some marking to do before I go to bed.'

His eyes queried that, but he said: 'Then as your headmaster, I'd better not detain you.'

It had been a warm day and the night was sweet. The sky, wine-dark, the moor indigo under a slim silver crescent of moon. At her door, Paul's amused glance was tinged with mystification. Eve felt as if she was being carefully weighed up.

He said, slowly and deliberately: 'I'm going to break my promise to you. I've decided not to stay in that square you've chalked out for me.'

With that, he put his arms round her and his lips came coaxingly down on hers. She drank in a little of the sweetness, and then resisted. Not because she wanted to; she wanted to drain the cup to the dregs — but because this mood that had overcome her was demanding recalcitrant action.

Unprovoked, Paul released her, and good-naturedly knuckled his hand down the side of her cheek. 'See you in the morning, my pixilated little friend,' he said, and continued jauntily up the street to his lodgings.

Humph! Pixilated indeed! Eve swung

her chin high in scarlet indignation, and stomped indoors.

It was her hope to sneak upstairs without falling foul of her mother's shrewd and knowing glance. She heard Clarissa Masters call out to her as she closed the door after herself, but deliberately misunderstood and called back: 'Yes, it's me, Mum. Goodnight.' And streaked up the stairs to her slope-roofed bedroom in the loft, flung open the bedroom door, and stopped.

In the short time she'd been out, the room had been stripped clean. She rushed about, opening cupboards and drawers. Clothes, books, perfume bottles and make-up pots, all the trivia and evidence of ownership had gone.

'That's what I was trying to tell you,' panted Clarissa Masters at the door, short of breath with the effort of running up the cruelly steep stairs. 'I've moved you into the spare room.' Always before she had called it the guest room, and her eyes lowered before the knowledge in Eve's. She twisted her fingers awkwardly. 'I couldn't put Shelley Anne in there.'

The austere measurements of the guest room aren't supposed to cramp me, then? To her credit, Eve never made this argumentative retort. Perhaps — at that — she was too deflated to do so. She simply brushed her lips against her mother's cheek and bid her an amenable good night.

As a child it had been her toys. Shelley Anne's penchant for boyish toys never stopped her acquisitive fingers from seizing Eve's dolls. Now it was her lovely lavender and white bedroom. Lavender walls; white bed with its puff-ball lavender duvet. Painstakingly planned, decorated and paid for by herself. The previous owner had had the spacious loft converted into a grandmother flat, only it hadn't worked out because the steps had proved too steep for elderly legs. Beyond the bedroom was a minute bathroom and an even smaller kitchen with a mini fridge and a cooker for scrambling eggs, cooking cheesey snacks and making late night cups of tea.

Prior to its conversion, the loft had been used as a storage place and the original outside staircase had been left intact, so that Eve was able to come and go as she pleased. Frequently, after spending the evening poring over school journals or marking papers, the need to stretch her cramped limbs and fill her lungs with air would take her to the door giving direct outside access, and no matter how late the hour she could take her walk without disturbing the household. This feeling of having privacy, the illusion of being able to shut the door on her own little world, assuaged her need for independence. Had circumstances been more favourable, Eve would have left home and be making her own way in the world. Having a place of her own within the home, was the next best thing.

Yet, as she plumped up the guest room pillow and lay her head down for sleep, her last conscious thoughts were not of the dolls that had been snatched from her arms, or even the bedroom that had been requisitioned. Her mind was filled with the chilling realisation that Shelley Anne was returning to blight her chances with Paul.

Could he, could any man, resist the bundle of restless energy moulded into the sensuous and riveting beauty of Shelley Anne?

3

Next morning Eve woke up feeling as silly as she felt repentant. She had judged the grown-up Shelley Anne on the exploits and waywardness of a child. And, anyway, even if Shelley Anne was still potential dynamite, was it just and fair to wish for anybody to be as dull and solemn as herself?

After that dramatic and totally untrue self-pronouncement, she leapt on top of the covers and, still kneeling on the bed, stuck her tongue out at the pale little face staring at her from the oval dressing-table mirror. More often than not, she saw herself in frowning, busy jerks, tugging her unruly hair or slapping moisturising cream on her cheeks to combat her love of walking in the wind. She was too much of a live spark, and far too modest anyway, to spare the time to stand and admire her ravishingly pretty chestnut hair, or take stock of eyes brilliant with infectious gaiety or filled with such a young and generous innocence that a man would be inspired to take up cudgels to protect their owner from the greed and dissipation of the world.

This morning the eyes were shadowed. So much so that her mother was compelled to ask most solicitously: 'Didn't you sleep well, pet?'

Eve resisted the temptation to snap back, 'I never do in a strange bed,' and said: 'Like a top.' Indeed her thoughts had been spinning like a top half the night.

Her father had already breakfasted, but accepted the offer of a second cup of tea to keep her company. Eve didn't really feel hungry and wished she'd stopped her mother serving up the usual cereal, egg, bacon and half a fried tomato, orange juice and toast. The portions were even larger this morning, as if her mother had needed to serve positive proof of her affection and appease her conscience at the same time.

Under her father's quizzical eye, Eve manfully waded through this feast, sneaking him a grateful smile when he helped her out by snaffling the toast. Although she favoured her mother in looks, Eve had always enjoyed a close relationship with her father. It was therefore not so strange that he, a normally unperceptive man, should be able to define some of the discord of her thoughts.

The time Eve had been set to leave home, it had been with his full approval. He had begged Eve to let his illness make no difference, and his wife had seconded this. But with such a feeble voice as to make Eve's going impossible. If Clarissa had been stronger in her convictions, had shown she was able to cope, Eve just might have been persuaded to go ahead with her plans. But his wife hadn't been strong, and had shown nothing but weakness, and so Eve had gone after a teaching post at Grange Lane Comprehensive, and settled to the work like a duck to water. Even taking Alice Meakin's petty bickering in her stride. Eve hadn't made much of a to-do about Alice Meakin's hostility to a new recruit, and though the poles would be nearer than those two could ever hope to get, Eve's sympathy for the senior teacher's narrow life seemed to be paying off and nowadays the friction was less apparent.

Ah well . . . William Masters was glad to interrupt this train of thought by bending his head to his newspaper. Minutes later his nose was coming up again and he was saying: 'Hey! What do you make of this? There's a fellow here in the paper who's had it acknowledged in Court that he's Pablo Vicente Alvérez's heir.' And he began to read from the newspaper, 'A certain young man, who wishes to remain anonymous, is at last acknowledged as heir to his famous grandfather's estate, following a long and hard legal battle.

He says it won't alter his way of life.'

'And who is, or I should say was, this Pablo whatever you said?'

'Only one of the best painters of our time. You might know him better as Pablo Alver.'

'Everybody's heard of Pablo Alver. Hasn't the value of his paintings increased dramatically since his death?'

'Yes. It's a sad but true fact that most great artists have attained almost unimaginable heights of fame and popularity when they are no longer around to appreciate it. His heir is reported as saying,' and her father started to read from the paper again, 'I have no intention of giving up a job which I like. Without a job, what are you? he asks. He goes on to say that he fought the case in the law courts out of principle, for the status of being the recognised grandson of Pablo Vicente Alvérez. M'mm. Despite all appeals, he refuses to reveal his identity.'

'What, no photograph of him? Not

even one of those barely recognisable smudges they sometimes show?'

'How could there be? A photo wouldn't do much for his anonymity.'

'Pity. I'd like to have seen what this most praiseworthy character looks like,' Eve commented drily. 'I bet it won't alter his way of life! I think . . . ' Catching sight of the clock out of the corner of her eye, speculation melted into disbelief. 'I think I'm going to be late. That can't be the time!'

'Five minutes fast, according to the radio time check.'

'Well, I suppose that's something,' she said, walking into the jacket her father thoughtfully reached for and held for her to slip her arms into. 'Thanks, Dad. Have a nice day. 'Bye.'

''Bye, love.'

★ ★ ★

William Masters watched his daughter run out of the house, and shook his head in amused tolerance. Would she ever slow down and adopt some grown-up poise? Leaving home would have done the trick. Her having to stay smote his heart, that faulty organ responsible for keeping her.

Eve was still in view of the window. He wondered why she didn't move on, and realised she was looking up the street, waiting for someone in her sight, but not in his, to catch up with her. Her voice was inaudible to him, but by reading the movements of her mouth and one swinging arm, he knew she was urging someone to, 'Come on! Put a sock in it, will you!'

The person Eve had been waiting for, caught up. He saw Paul Smalley take his daughter's arm, and watched the two of them march companionably down the street. He thought idly that it would be nice to see his Eve settled with a good man of her own.

'You get later, Miss Masters.'

'Pan calling the kettle, Mr Smalley?' Eve retaliated, smiling perkily up at Paul. 'If you suddenly came into money, would you opt out?'

'What on earth are you talking about?'

'Fellow in the paper this morning. Dad read it out to me. Got it proved in Court that he's the grandson of Pablo Vicente Alvérez, which must be worth a thousand or two. The painter, you know.' In case Paul didn't recognise the famous painter and lesser known sculptor with the 'Vicente' bit included and the 'ez' added to the instantly recognisable Alver.

'I did know,' teased Paul. 'I'm not an absolute moron.'

'Sorry. Anyway, this gentleman, who refuses to reveal his identity, said to the effect that any monetary gain would come second to the status of proving — his legitimacy I suppose. And he says he's not packing in his job. Would you?'

'How do you know there was a monetary gain? Court cases can cost as well as make a packet. And would I what?'

Eve gave a little sigh of exasperation. 'You are being deliberately provocative.'

'That makes a change. That's the ploy you use on me.'

Ignoring the warm confusion trickling up from her neck, because she didn't for a moment think he seriously thought that, although she passionately wished he found her as tantalising as the lively flicker in his eye was making out, she said: 'It's almost as if you were stalling deliberately.'

Again she found herself floundering before the brilliance of his look, which was made up of nine parts sparkling mischief. Oddly, it was the tenth part which was tenderness that disconcerted her most.

'Have you thought that could be your fault?'

Her throat was too constricted to ask why. He spared her the necessity by continuing smoothly: 'Perhaps you haven't asked me the right question.'

'You don't want to give an answer,' she said gruffly.

'You reckon? What would you say if I told you you'd hit the nail on the head?'

He was teasing her and he was not teasing her; her confusion was such that she couldn't tell which. 'I haven't the slightest idea what you're getting at.'

His expression stilled and grew serious. She had to strain her ears to catch his reply, it was so soft. 'Perhaps I am the grandson of Pablo Vicente Alvérez, only I don't want it known. Yet because I cannot lie to you, I'm being deliberately evasive.'

She gasped. It was the most incredible thing she'd heard. And yet . . . she was now remembering seeing an earlier report, in the same daily. At the very beginning of the court case, the paper had carried a more lengthy account. The sons of Pablo Alver's brothers had questioned the validity of the claim on legitimacy grounds. They said the famous painter had never married his English sweetheart. At the back of Eve's mind was the memory of a press photograph of a sweet old lady brandishing her marriage certificate. She was reported as saying . . . oh what was it? . . . if only memory could be commanded. Ah! it was coming to her now. Her daughter and her English son-in-law were both dead, but their son, her grandson who was named for his famous grandfather, must search the records and clear the family good name. That would make the grandson a good few parts English, having an English father and a mother born of an English mother.

She slid a glance at Paul and froze because of . . . the name! Named for his grandfather, Pablo Vicente Alvérez. Paul in Spanish was Pablo. Certainly Paul looked English, but at the same time his skin was dark enough to have Latin forebears. And something else . . . she remembered this with a prickly cold excitement. Paul had a middle name beginning with a V. And on top of that he'd said, 'Perhaps I am the grandson of

Pablo Vicente Alvérez.' Hadn't the name, not universally associated with the world famous Pablo Alver, rolled too smoothly off his tongue? Would he have remembered it so accurately from hearing her mention it just the once?

She had almost convinced herself that Paul was really Pablo Alver's heir, and was ready to burst with happiness at Paul's amazing good fortune when, just in time to stop her from making a fool of herself, she noticed the pronounced twinkle in his eye, and the morning newspaper protruding from his pocket!

The unfamiliar name had slid effortlessly from his tongue because obviously he'd read all about the case; and just as obviously he was sending her up!

'Paul Smalley!' The tense concentration her features had been cemented into, dissolved, and mirth reshaped her mouth. 'You're too wicked for words. You'd say anything for a laugh.'

And a laugh it got. Then, and at odd-moments during the day when it popped into her mind to enliven a dull history lesson and the duller aftermath of marking during her free period. And at other moments her eyes misted with dreams as she thought how wonderful if it had been true. It would be something to be the grand-daughter-in-law of Pablo Alver, the celebrated painter and sculptor.

A thought of pure bliss sent a tremor glancing down her spine.

It would be even more wonderful to be the wife of Paul Smalley, schoolmaster, who wore a tweed jacket with leather-bound cuffs and leather elbow patches, had a delicious sense of humour and who strayed too often into her thoughts for . . . efficiency.

Ruefully she changed the cross for a trick on a pupil's perfectly correct answer.

She wondered what the middle initial in Paul's name stood for. V for Vernon? Valentine? Vaughan? Vincent . . . for the Spanish Vicente? Oh no . . . she wasn't going to start all that up again.

★ ★ ★

Several days later, Eve found it necessary to say: 'Paul? Can I sneak off as soon as the bell goes this afternoon?'

'Heavy date?' His tone was teasing, with a light salting of speculation.

Heavy heart, Eve thought. She shood her head. 'I'm meeting Shelley Anne's train.'

'Shanks's pony?' She could have borrowed her father's car, but he hadn't noticed it in the parking area in the playground.

'There at least. Unfortunately, Dad's car's in dock. We'll need to take a taxi back to convey the masses of luggage my cousin will think it necessary to bring for even a short stay.'

'How about if I give you a lift in my car? I can nip to my lodgings and fetch it at break.' He didn't come to school in his car because he maintained the journey was too short to warrant it, and anyway he liked the exercise.

'Lovely,' Eve accepted joylessly. Silly

46

of her, but she'd wanted to keep Shelley Anne and Paul apart for as long as possible.

She didn't feel at all put out when an irate parent claimed Paul late in the afternoon. Paul found time to slide his face round her classroom door to say: 'Sorry. It seems I shall be detained. Might not be for long, if you want to hang on.'

'I won't, thanks all the same.' And now she had difficulty in not looking too pleased.

All day the sky had had that heavy look that betokens rain, but now the grey had started to roll away to reveal pellucid patches of pale blue. Not only was this chequered effect pretty, but an errant shaft of sunshine found its way into the classroom. The archaic stained-glass window cast a rosy glow over the rows of desks. Rosy was the expression on her pupils faces at the near-promise of the home-time bell.

Eve wasted no time in joining the home-going torrent that poured out of the school to block the pavement. The string of colourful cars waiting to take children to outlying districts resembled tawdry jewels in a street setting that was Victorian, and as narrow as the morals of that era.

A car window was hurriedly wound down. A blonde head, a screaming ball of mimosa, poked out. 'Miss Masters, have you a second?'

'I'm sorry, but I haven't, Mrs Brookes.'

'I wanted to talk to you about Charlotte,' Lilith Brookes said pettishly.

As if Eve hadn't already guessed that. Charlotte had been the form's brightest promise. The remarriage of her father had turned Charlotte's lively, seeking scholarly mind inward into indifference. Eve knew as well as anybody that it was only a matter of time before this indifference found a mischievous outlet. Somebody ought to make Charlotte see her stepmother wasn't the monster her vivid imagination had created. But Eve felt she wasn't capable of dealing with this tricky situation.

All the same, she would have stayed and talked had time permitted.

'I really am sorry, Mrs Brookes, but I'm meeting my cousin's train and I should have been at the station five minutes ago.'

'Don't let me keep you a moment longer,' was Lilith Brookes' icy reply.

'Another time?' Eve suggested diffidently.

Lilith's husband was a personal friend of Paul's. She didn't want Paul coming back at her, asking what she had done to upset his friend's wife.

Lilith Brookes slid back across the passenger seat to her position behind the driving wheel. She didn't bother to answer Eve.

As Eve walked away, out of the tail of her eye she saw Charlotte approach the car with dragging feet. She sighed. There might be another time for a discussion with Lilith Brookes about Charlotte, but how could she voice an unbiased opinion when it took her all her time to keep a civil tongue in her head? That woman rubbed her up the wrong way.

Much as she suspected, Shelley Anne's train was already in. As Eve hadn't seen her cousin for a good number of years, she did wonder if recognition would be instantaneous. Her eye alighted on a tall, glamorous figure in a white trouser suit sitting detached and unruffled amid a mountain of luggage, and she knew she need search no further.

Shelley Anne's hair hung in a black tassel to her shoulder blades. Her roll-neck, peppery pimento red sweater accentuated her tiny pointed chin and small straight nose. Some say characters are best read in the unguarded expression of the eyes. The drawback to this is that a really true glance can be fleeting and one must be quick to catch it, also anyone cunning enough could off-set a too revealing look. The physical shape of the mouth is often a better guide.

Shelley Anne's mouth was small and as tightly contained as a rose bud. It laughed more than it sulked, but this was because Shelley Anne had learnt at an early age how to get her own way, and she had acquired the knack of salvaging fun out of disaster. It was a mouth capable of cunning.

It seemed to Eve that Shelley Anne's face had shrunk. The tender crescents beneath her eyes looked bruised despite her golden tan, and her black-diamond eyes lacked their remembered lustre. A sharp reminder that Shelley Anne was supposed to have been involved in a car crash. While admitting that Shelley Anne looked ill, Eve wondered at herself for thinking in terms of 'supposed'.

'Hello, Shelley Anne. Sorry I'm late.'

Shelley Anne's eyes came up in a slow, unbothered fashion. 'I knew you'd come.' Her mouth shaped derisively round 'Dear, dependable Eve.' But she only spoke her cousin's name out loud. 'As a matter of fact, life's been pelting at me lately. It was nice to sit and be lazy while waiting for somebody to come and pick me up. Do you ever get weary, Eve? Of the constant go of living, and having to make decisions?'

'Can we split this lot up?' said Eve, coming to a decision about the accumulation of three suitcases, two canvas holdalls, a plastic carrier sprouting shoes, and another one bulging with records and books, strewn at their feet. Shelley Anne might have invited herself for a short stay, but Eve was an Indian squaw if this lot didn't amount to Shelley Anne's total possessions.

'I'll take the two heaviest suitcases and a holdall, if you can . . . '

'Any transport laid on?' Shelley Anne enquired practically.

'No. Paul was going to drive me here. Unfortunately at the last minute he was detained, but we should get a taxi.'

'Paul is?' The long tassel of hair floated to one side as Shelley Anne held her head at a speculative angle. 'I was going to hazard a guess that he was your special man, but he's not worthy of that honour if he lets anything keep him from your side.'

'It isn't a question of being kept from my side, but more that he's a job to do.'

'Which he does with great dedication, I'm sure. You haven't denied that he's your special man,' teased the tight little mouth.

'I haven't affirmed it, either,' said Eve sickly, as the damning colour flooded her cheeks. 'Paul is Headmaster of Grange Lane Comprehensive where I teach.' She was kicking herself for not being more subtle.

'A schoolmaster,' mocked Shelley Anne, patently losing interest. 'Chalk under his finger nails and leather patches on his jacket.'

It was so near the truth that despite herself Eve felt the primness of her mouth relaxing in a smile. 'Well, yes . . . Would you rather I leave you here with the luggage and go find a taxi and come back for you?'

Shelley Anne gave Eve a brief assessing stare and frowned her judgement. 'At the last event, dearie.' Unkindly intimating just what she thought Eve's chances were. 'Acquiring a taxi requires a special talent and even making allowances for . . . ' As she spoke her eyes were flicking hopefully round the station, and almost as if he was on a line being played in, a personable man sauntered down the platform from the direction of the refreshment buffet.

A stranger to Eve, so presumably also to Shelley Anne and the town. He had darkish green-grey flecked eyes, a colour beloved of artists in turbulent seascapes, dark hair fashionably cut, a colourful, faintly Bohemian taste in clothes. A purple jacket, but in a subdued shade of purple that blended with the silver and grey shadow stripe in his trousers.

Both girls were looking at this very lookable-at stranger. Eve had no idea that one of them was going to speak to him until Shelley Anne jumped up and put herself in his path. To save trampling her down, a hand went to her shoulder, liked the feel of it there and was in no hurry to pull it away.

Shelley Anne fluttered her long lashes. It should have looked false, contrived, even theatrical. It didn't. She appealed blatantly: 'Excuse me. I'm terribly sorry to trouble you, but could you help us?'

Anything short of jumping from the Victorian ironwork under the train coming in on platform two, Eve thought wryly.

'The thing is — ' Charmingly, Shelley Anne bit her underlip. 'My cousin has just arrived with this calamitous amount of luggage,' she lied. 'Would you . . . ? I do hate to ask but . . . '

How she could lie in her teeth and still retain that guileless look of flower-like innocence was beyond Eve's credibility.

'Don't move. My car is garaged not

far from here. I'll fetch it and pull it right to the station entrance.' His eyes made small work of Shelley Anne's vast amount of luggage. 'Soon have that shifted.

'It's very kind of you to assist us,' said Shelley Anne.

'Not at all. The pleasure is all mine,' he gallantly responded.

It happened as easily and as effortlessly as if it had been pre-rehearsed.

'I just wish you'd been outside the school to deal with a certain pupil's stepmother,' said Eve, both envious and resentful as the stranger walked away.

'What's that?'

'How could you do it? What was the point of that stupid lie? And now I know what's been puzzling me and that is how you managed to get all this luggage on the train in the first place. Obviously another accommodating mug obliged. And what if this one had known me? Don't forget you're playing on my home ground now.' The fact that he'd got a car garaged nearby proved he wasn't the absolute stranger to the town Eve had taken him to be. 'You were taking a chance, weren't you?'

There wasn't much joy to be found in ticking off Shelley Anne, because she had acquired the knack of not taking a telling off seriously. A vague and disconcerting memory of a much younger Shelley Anne saying, 'The best weapon of retaliation is laughter,' popped into Eve's mind.

Shelley Anne's delicious smile dove-tailed nicely with her wheedling tone. 'Come on, it wasn't much of a chance. I could tell by the look on your face that you didn't know Lover Boy any more than — 'Her teeth caught her underlip and her smile grew more provocative — 'I did. Don't pretend to be cross, sweetie. Just concentrate hard on the fact that Shelley Anne has arrived to make life easy for you. The memory I've always stored of you is of an aggressive do-it-yourselfer. You make a profession of making life difficult for yourself. You haven't changed a bit. Now tell me what you think of me in my trendy white suit! Do you think I've changed at all?'

Sincerity and wide-eyed innocence a smoke screen for perfidity and lies, oodles of charm and a zest for living!

Eve shook her head helplessly. 'Not at all. You haven't changed one iota.'

'In whatever context that was said, I regard it as a compliment.' The black eyes twinkled. 'Insensitive, that's me, despite the label to the contrary which I drape round my delectable neck.'

Well of course Shelley Anne would know of the sincerity she oozed.

Suddenly Shelley Anne's eyes grew serious, and there was more than just the warmth of personal contact in the hand that reached out to curl round Eve's wrist. There was — or was Eve being as bamboozled as everybody else? — affection.

Ironically, what Shelley Anne chose to say was: 'You're about the only person I've never been able to fool,

Eve. You've always been able to see right through me and, in a way, I'm not sorry. With you I can relax and be my own detestable self. Beneath the sweet surface I'm as vile as they come.'

Eve found her own expression going thoughtful. 'That's the way I've always seen you, but I've just had a startling thought.'

'Stamp on it,' said Eve with swift perception.

'No . . . I think the hardness the top layer of sweetness covers is just a skin. Peel that off and I believe you're so soft underneath that you're made of sponge.'

'All this talk of peeling, as if I'm an onion. Listen, the only likeness I have to an onion is that I make other people weep. You're bonkers, you must be. You know your trouble, you tend to sift everything through logic.'

'Is that so bad?'

'It is when you're as way off the mark

59

as you are now. Look, Lover Boy is coming back.'

Eve had a definite notion that the conversation had touched a nerve and Shelley Anne was glad it had to be abandoned for the present. Not being far behind the door when intelligence was given out, Eve had an idea that next time, if she ever managed to broach the subject again, Shelley Anne would be better prepared.

'My car's just outside,' announced Lover Boy. 'No — ' As Eve made to swing up a suitcase — 'You girls aren't to lift a thing. I should be able to do it at twice. You lovely ladies can stand guard and accompany me on the last trip. Mind if we delay introductions until everything's safely stowed in the car, because I've slightly more than a suspicion that I'm parked in a no-parking area.

Eve's expression was more than a little agonised. Some people can't take chances in life. They've only to pass through Customs with a gulp of booze above the duty free allowance and they get pinched. Eve belonged to this category. Shelley Anne couldn't see what Eve was getting fussed about. She double parked, flagrantly exceeded the speed limit and thought everybody fiddled their tax returns as a matter of course. She rarely got caught in anything. She never consciously thought of coming a cropper.

Eve's fears proved groundless, and she found herself and most of Shelley Anne's luggage occupying the cramped back seat of a car that was most definitely not in the luxury class.

Shelley Anne gave the address, and prodded Eve into giving brief instructions how to get there.

'Introductions now, do you think? I'm Shelley Anne Masters.' She tossed her black hair. 'The black sheep of the family. I always confess that at the onset and then the shock isn't too great. This — ' waving a hand — 'is my cousin, Eve Masters, a much better bet in every way. Sterling qualities has our Eve. Now you.'

'Peregrine Anthony Adamson,' he said.

'That's an extravagant mouthful of name to swallow, but it suits you,' said Shelley Anne. She smiled engagingly. 'Shall I call you Perry or Tony?'

'My sweet old gran calls me Peregrine, but I'm honestly a lot happier answering to Tony. What do I call you?'

'I'm always called Shelley Anne.'

'Nobody ever brought you down to size?'

'People have tried. Nobody ever has.'

Eve felt superfluous in the back.

'Where do you roost, Tony?' Shelley Anne enquired. 'And is there a Mrs Adamson in the nest?'

Eve had to admire how effortlessly her cousin asked all the relevant questions. But what had Eve really gasping was the spontaneity between the two. They were striking sparks off each other as if they were old sparring partners and not new acquaintances.

'I'm not married,' said Tony.

'What, a fine looking man like you? Don't tell me the girls aren't queuing up!'

Despite her confusion (spelt red cheeks) Eve found herself smiling at the neat way Tony's humour capped Shelley Anne's as he adroitly replied, skimming Eve a look over his shoulder: 'The fact is, this Son of Adam has never met the Eve he'd be prepared to forgo his freedom for.'

Eve's confusion was ripening nicely; Shelley Anne's coolness said she was not amused. As Tony Adamson started to slow down the car, Eve had cause to say: 'We don't live here.'

'No, I do,' Tony replied. 'I was just pointing out where I lived. The house with the yellow door.'

'That was old Lettie Lomas's cottage,' said Eve conjecturally as they picked up speed. 'It was supposedly let to an artist, but it's remained closed up and nobody's seen hide or hair of him.'

'I do dabble in paint a bit,' he replied in what Eve thought must be a rare moment of modesty, because he gave the impression of being an immodest, flamboyant character. 'I rented the place, dumped my things, and then had to return to London to see to a spot of unfinished business.'

'Which I trust you concluded satisfactorily,' said Shelley Anne in a funny, held-back voice, as if she found it a source of great amusement. But that didn't make sense.

Any more than the forbidding edge of Tony's face visible to her through the driving mirror. He looked quite stern. Eve puzzled over what Shelley Anne had said, but she couldn't find anything in her cousin's innocuous remark about hoping he'd concluded his business satisfactorily that could turn his good humour into frowning displeasure. Yet Tony looked, was this fanciful of her, but — goaded.

Tony didn't deliver them and drive straight away, although Eve got the impression this is what he would have preferred doing. But charmingly concurred with her suggestion to come in and meet her parents.

William Masters was prompt in his thanks. Surveying the amount of luggage he said he didn't see how the girls could have managed without Tony's help. Tony once again said he'd been happy to be of assistance, and accepted Clarissa Masters' invitation to stay to tea.

Eve thought he must be working it out that she, as the daughter of the house, was its permanent occupant and not Shelley Anne as he might have been led to believe. Shelley Anne's senseless lie was bound to be uncovered. Eve couldn't understand why her cousin had lied in the first place. What did it matter which of them had just got off the train? Shelley Anne was either a compulsive liar, or she thought it looked inelegant to be travelling with that vast amount of clutter. Wasn't the ultimate in sophistication having the requirements for any situation in one suitcase?

'Did you say you travelled down with Shelley Anne, Mr Adamson?' Clarissa Masters enquired in all innocence as she brought in the tea tray. 'Set the table up, love,' she told Eve. 'I don't think the small trolley will hold this lot. Tell me, Mr Adamson, did you get acquainted with Shelley Anne on the train, or did you two know each other before?'

Tony seemed to take a long time in replying, and first he said, 'Thank you,' for the cup of tea placed within reach of his hand. Then he said: 'I discovered Eve and Shelley Anne sitting on a platform bench surrounded by luggage. My car was within easy reach, so I was pleased to offer them a lift. It has occurred to me since that I must have been on the same train.'

That was all right as far as it went. But shouldn't Tony have questioned which girl was on the train?

Chancing to look in Eve's direction, and seeing the puzzled look on her face, set Tony's thoughts into deeper tracks. It didn't take him long to pin that look down, but wouldn't it be the gallant thing to smother his consternation and say nothing? His narrowing eyes fell on Shelley Anne. It was not up to him to expose her lie.

Intercepting the eye play between Eve and Tony, and feeling herself now the victim of his glance, Shelley Anne turned it into something or nothing by saying: 'All right, so I lied. But it was only a teeny lie and if you think about it a very natural one.' Turning all her appealing repentance on her aunt, she said: 'You see, Aunt Clarissa, there I was with all this luggage, wondering how I could enlist help. You know how difficult it is to ask for help for oneself. So was it very wrong of me to bend the truth just a little and ask for help on Eve's behalf?'

'Did you?' Glancing at Tony, Clarissa Masters said: 'I'm sure that was a very unnecessary subterfuge. But I know what you mean. It's like collecting for charity. One can be quite brazen when it's not for personal gain.' Clarissa Masters shook her head with affectionate tolerance. Shelley Anne was obviously as zany as ever.

But Eve was not as easily satisfied. She was convinced the lie had a more sinister purpose. And she wasn't sure that Tony was the one meant to be hoodwinked.

4

As soon as Tony went, Shelley Anne's luggage was humped up the first flight of stairs, and then up the second steeper flight to her new quarters, the self-contained flatlet that had been the joy of Eve's existence.

Shelley Anne's profile was alert with delighted disbelief. 'You're not putting me here? Oh, how super!' And she darted hither and thither like an entranced but well-schooled child. Acquisitive fingers curled into the palms of her hands, not touching while anybody was looking, but sampling everything with her eyes until they shone so much they were in danger of splitting with ecstasy.

But was she really this pleased with the premises, or was she exalting over possession? Why did a picture fling itself into Eve's mind of Shelley Anne quite delirious with delight over a doll taken from Eve? Not delighting in the doll, which would have been a natural childish reaction, but over the moon because she'd taken it from Eve.

Shelley Anne crossed to the wide window which yielded a commanding view of the wild stretch of moor. Eve liked it best in storm, its sombre blackness bleached brilliant white as fork-lighting cracked overhead, or when the wind blew hard enough to inspire the heather to look and sound like a screaming sea swell. Ravens overhead and not gulls, a rolling foam of heather and not a restless rise and fall of waves!

Today, not to frighten Shelley Anne but to welcome her, the moor had put on a sunny face. The merest breath of wind stirred fat, fleecy clouds in soporific motion across a blue sky.

Shelley Anne swung round to face Eve, her hands going together under her pointed chin. 'This is your room. How can you bear to give this up? Do you mind terribly having to give it up to me?'

Clarissa Masters knew her daughter too well to allow her to reply. Honesty and not social kindness would govern Eve's words. Eve hadn't yet learnt there are times when even the most righteous person must parry the truth. So she said quickly: 'Dear Shelley Anne, it's a small sacrifice on Eve's part in comparison to the pleasure she'll have in your company.'

'Now I know why you're my favourite aunt,' Shelley Anne said sweetly.

Eve played with a jagged thumb nail. She'd caught it while helping to carry up Shelley Anne's luggage, and hadn't had time to file it smooth again. She wished it were possible to file herself smooth. She wished she didn't feel so raw and torn. Only a small mean mind could resent Shelley Anne so much.

But Shelley Anne had always had much more than her. Better-off parents, so much more money to splash around on clothes. Exciting jobs. Exotic travel to places that were just names in a geography text book to Eve. Was it very wrong of her to resent the intrusion on her small-by-comparison preserves?

Clarissa Masters said: 'You look tired, Shelley Anne. Sort of bruised round the eyes. But on the whole, I'm pleased to see you looking as well as this after your . . . I believe you said in your letter you were involved in a car accident?'

'Yes, Aunt Clarissa.'

Clarissa Masters waited expectantly, and with a small resigned sigh, Shelley Anne went on: 'I was travelling in this car with a friend. We were . . . '

'Do you find the telling too painful?' said Clarissa Masters gently.

'Thank you, Aunt Clarissa, but I can tell you. We were involved in a pile-up on the motorway in thick fog.'

'Terrible, dear. How I sympathise. It's a strange time of year to have fogs,' she puzzled. 'We haven't had any up here.'

'It wasn't a fog . . . more of a heat

mist. It was scarey. Being in a situation and having no control over events. The medical report said I escaped unhurt, but I don't think I'll ever be the same again. Afterwards, I felt too shook up to concentrate on my work or anything. Couldn't eat, barely nibbled at my food, couldn't sleep. I just had this urge to pack up and leave my job and my flat, both of which I'd adored before. Only I couldn't think of anywhere to go, and then I thought of you.'

'Child, I'm so glad you did,' soothed Clarissa Masters. 'I'm upsetting you, so no more talk. Anything you need, anything at all, just ask. And now I'll leave you. Eve will stay and help you unpack.'

'That would be nice.'

Eve felt rather than saw the glance darted at her. Out of the tail of her eye she saw Shelley Anne run to her mother and bend down, because Shelley Anne was the taller by several inches, and very gently, very gratefully and very effectively, kiss Clarissa Masters on the cheek. It was a throat-clogging, sincere performance. So why did Eve get the impression that Shelley Anne had never been involved in a car accident? That the pile-up in thick fog, or heat-mist, or whatever she chose to call it, had not occurred outside the devious tracks of her mind, and that she had been play-acting from start to finish.

Shelley Anne was still enjoying her look-about, making a pig of herself with her eyes. She had enough savvy to wait until Clarissa Masters had gone before she put on a gloating smile to say: 'Aunt Clarissa mentioned you'd moved out for me. That's how I knew this was your room. It's self-contained, like a flat.'

'That was the idea. The people who had the house before us called it the grandmother flat. They went to all the bother of having it converted, and then found the access was too steep for their grandmother. Otherwise it was perfect. All the facilities for privacy in the bosom of the family.'

'Yes,' mused Shelley Anne. 'I'm going to enjoy this. I'll invite you up for a late-night coffee session some time,' she said impishly. 'I suppose,' she continued on a slightly bored note, 'we'd better get on with the tedious job of unpacking. I'd prefer to leave it, but — '

'But?' prompted Eve.

The light of devilment was like a homing pigeon that returned to Shelley Anne's eye. 'Don't want to upset Aunt Clarissa at the onset by drawing attention to my sloth.'

This provided Eve with a possible clue. She took a deep breath and dared: 'Is that why you invented the road accident?'

Because she was closely watching for Shelley Anne's reaction, Eve didn't miss the startled gasp, although it was checked instantly, swallowed into drawling indifference. 'What do you mean? Why should I invent that?'

No going back now. On, all the way

to downfall, vowed Eve. 'To draw out this visit as long as possible. Because Mother and Dad only know what it is to be hard-working and industrious and they wouldn't be able to understand anybody idling about at their expense unless they were ill.'

'Quick, aren't you?' said Shelley Anne, springing the lock on the first suitcase and starting to take things out.

'Am I?' Eve folded undies into a drawer. 'I was rather hoping I'd be on the wrong track. It's not pleasant to see your parents fooled by lies.'

'What are you going to do about it?'

'Nothing. I'm not your conscience. You're not putting the onus of that on me.'

Shelley Anne saw that although Eve's mouth was in a rigid line, she was not angry, only deeply upset. 'Would it make it any better in your eyes if I told you it wasn't all lies? That although there was no car accident, no pile-up in thick fog, quite a large chunk of what I said was true.'

'Try me.'

'No collision in thick fog. But every bit as scarey, believe me.' Shelley Anne caught at her lower lip in agitation, drawing a pin-prick of blood.

'If you don't want . . . ' began Eve, regretting stumbling on something pain-giving and private. Because hadn't she decided earlier that Shelley Anne was sponge underneath and while she hadn't minded banging ineffectually on the solid outer coating, she found it disconcerting to feel her claws sinking into the vulnerable soft centre.

'Funnily enough, I do want . . . to tell you. Not all, not the meaty details, just the bare bones of finding myself in a situation and having no control over events. I was in a fog all right, a fog of circumstance, and a pile-up, a pile-up of emotions. A medical report would say I escaped unhurt, but I spoke the truth when I said that about not eating and being unable to concentrate, and knowing I won't ever be the same again. Blast him, I don't even like him!'

She tore her fingernails down the front of her trouser suit, as if she wanted to tear him from her breast. Her voice was unattractive and harsh. 'I don't like what he is, what he stands for or anything about him. But I'm powerless to resist the animal attraction he was over me.'

A man! Of course, it would be a man.

'It would be just the same if I were tied up with someone else with a houseful of kids. He'd only have to whistle and I'd run to him.'

'You aren't married and you haven't any children. So what's the problem? Isn't he free?'

'Would that make any difference to me? If he were married the problem wouldn't be unresolvable. I could take him away from another woman. I know what you're thinking and it does sound contemptible, but the truth is and so I avoid it as much as possible. You are the instigator of this George Washington line of conversation, not I, so don't you dare cringe away from it. I know the score. I know I'm attractive enough and unscrupulous enough to take a man away from a woman in a straight fight, with no other issue at stake. Perhaps it's because I've never had anybody to deal with like him before, but I don't know how to separate him from his rottenness. He was born rotten, but it doesn't make any difference. So you see what sort of a mess I am, and what sort of mess I'm in.'

'Shouldn't that be was in? You're talking as if it's a situation that's still active and not one you've skipped out of.'

'Am I? How strange!' Her laugh was unconvincing. Something else for Eve to ponder on later.

They had unpacked as they'd talked. Eve felt herself relenting. 'That's one suitcase dealt with. Would you prefer to leave unpacking the others until later?'

'I would please.'

'I'll push off then.'

A ghost of a smile whisked up the corners of Shelley Anne's mouth. 'Bless you. I feel exhausted. Will you tell Aunt Clarissa I'm going to lie down. Perhaps I'll sleep.'

'Of course. It will do you good. I'll tell Mother you would prefer not to be disturbed, and we'll leave it to you to come down when you're hungry. Just one thing before I go, may I borrow that newspaper?'

'Which newspaper?'

'The one lining the suitcase we've just unpacked.'

'Oh that one! It's a Spanish newspaper. I brought it home as a . . . a sort of souvenir last time I visited my parents. You wouldn't be able to read it.' She went to sit on the bed, drawing her legs up and closing the suitcase lid with her toe.

'I suppose not,' Eve replied accommodatingly now the newspaper was effectively removed from her sight. 'I still only know snatches of Spanish, despite following a series of Spanish language programmes on the radio.'

'It's much easier to pick up the language when you're out there.'

'Yes. So they say. Are Uncle Richard and Aunt Dorothy still in that restaurant venture?'

'At the moment. My parents are very expensive people, and it's not quite the get rich quick thing they imagined, but they find the life compatible.'

'Your parents are very adventurous, aren't they?'

'If you mean they are still seeking the pot of gold at the end of the rainbow, that they haven't yet discovered the simple joy of settling down, then yes they are adventurous. I don't think I can ever remember a time when they were not bubbling over with some scheme that was going to reap them a fortune overnight. The places we've been . . .'

'Yes,' said Eve, just a little enviously. 'When did you say you visited your parents last?'

'Fairly recently.'

'How recently?' said Eve, not knowing why she persisted.

'A couple of months back.'

It was later, in the narrowness of her new room, that Eve's thoughts closed on two things. Had there been a trace of wistfulness in Shelley Anne's tone as she'd spoken of her parents' restless wanderings? And what was in a two month old Spanish newspaper that was important enough to make Shelley Anne take pains not to let Eve see?

But right then Eve went downstairs to tell her mother that Shelley Anne was resting and to offer her services because it was getting on for suppertime.

Father, mother and daughter ate. Shelley Anne had failed to answer a light tap on the door, so was presumed asleep. It was a casserole meal, so hers was left in a slow oven. Eve helped with the washing up, then excused herself to go upstairs to do some marking. Unlike her old room, this room was too narrow and confining. She opened the window, but still she felt stifled. If she could have worked she would have put up with it, but concentration was like a greasy rope that kept slipping from her grasp. Realising the futility of continuing in her present mood, she went to the wardrobe for her coat, kicked off her bedroom mules and laced her feet into sensible walking shoes.

Her mother's raised eyebrows at her reappearance underlined how much she was going to miss the free movement her outside staircase had provided.

'I feel a bit, stuffed up,' she explained. 'Won't be long. Just going for a stroll to blow away the cobwebs.' Lucky Shelley Anne, who could come and go without the need to tell.

It was not that Eve minded explaining her movements to her mother, she had nothing to hide; what she felt was more of an irritation at having a prized freedom suddenly curtailed.

Automatically, she walked down towards the Elephant and Castle, rather than up in the direction of the moor. The moor held no fear for her at any time, not when the wind funnelled at her from the east, or the rain teamed its black vengeance on her often uncovered head. So on a kind night such as it was, it would have been pleasant to stride up its moon-blanched back. The attraction of the opposite direction was that there was more chance of bumping into Paul in the vicinity of the Elephant and Castle. The homely lounge bar being a cosier prospect than the chill formality of his landlady's parlour. He said he'd rather look at people than a flight of plaster ducks.

Eve had seen the ducks, flying across Mrs Taylor's parlour wall. Even in their heyday she couldn't imagine them looking decorative. They were nasty, unattractive and cheap. Of Victorian vintage, Paul had said they not only looked cheap but were cheap to make. Not because of their simplicity of design and manufacture, but because like as not they'd been produced by child labour. He'd come up with some figure then. Something about a child of nine working a seventy hour week and being expected to make some 145,000 of these revolting figures for the princely wage per year of — and then he'd stopped his text-book quotings, laughed and said: 'What's five guineas in decimal currency?'

'Everything is different these days,' she'd said. 'Even the money.'

'No,' he'd said. 'Some things are the same. Child labour is still exploited.'

It wasn't difficult to know what he meant. To appease the Money Goddess, some parents still drove their children to unendurable lengths. In her class alone, there was a boy who had a paper round every morning and humped heavy crates and boxes in the local supermarket every evening. Consequently, he fell asleep over his books. Another child, a girl this time, was frequently absent from school because she had so many household chores to do. When questioned about this the mother had puffed up with indignation and righteously replied: 'Well, someone has got to do the cleaning up. You'd have something to say if our Cheryl was living in a midden, wouldn't you? And I'm out at work all day.'

Charlotte Brookes, the step-daughter of the woman who had accosted Eve earlier, was a different sort of problem altogether. Charlotte's father was a company director and they lived in a luxury, stone-built house on the other side of the moor. No one expected such a vital, attractive man to remain a widower. And from a business point of view, Lilith was the perfect helpmate. She had been a top-flight secretary, not quite a Mistress Mind, but high enough in intelligence to be able to talk knowledgeably to her successful husband's friends and business acquaintances. She sparkled as a hostess, but was falling down miserably as a mother. Charlotte needed a mother's understanding and guidance more desperately than the most deprived child in Eve's class. The material advantages her father piled on her was forcing a chasm between the wretched 'favoured' child and her jealous classmates.

At this juncture in her thought ramblings, Eve arrived at the Elephant and Castle. Peeping through the leaded bow window, she saw Paul sitting at a corner table, a meat pie (his supper?) and a tankard of beer in front of him. He looked up, saw her, and made an exaggerated hand movement for her to come and join him. She back-tracked to swing through the door; her walk was jaunty. Every step that took her nearer to Paul seemed to get lighter.

As soon as she was settled with her usual shandy, Paul said without preamble: 'Nick Brookes rang me up. What have you been doing to upset his missus?'

Not exactly an unexpected turn-up in her gone-wrong day. But because she had expected this, did not mean that she had prepared for it.

'She jumped me as I was leaving school.'

'She said you were so sharp off the mark you beat the kids out.'

'That's unjust, and you know it. I told you I had to get to the station to meet my cousin's train. I hope you told Nick Brookes that there are more evenings when I'm not so sharp off the mark.'

He met her flaring temper with cool amusement. 'Keep your hair on, that's precisely what I told him.'

'It wasn't that I didn't want to discuss Charlotte with her Ma.' Eve thought she'd better get that one in. At the same time she wriggled with just a feather tickle of unease because at first, until Paul had made her see the situation in fairer perspective, she hadn't shown the Charlotte problem the sympathy she felt for a materially deprived child. Perhaps at the bottom of her she was no better than any of Charlotte's jealous classmates. Her own position in life was finely balanced somewhere between the haves and the have-nots, and she found it difficult to pity a child who had everything.

'Stepmother,' Paul's cool tone was dynamite packed.

'What's that?' queried Eve with a lively light in her eye.

'You said Charlotte's Ma. I corrected you. Step-Ma. There lies the vital difference.'

'Yes,' agreed Eve. It was a case of being wrong again. Charlotte didn't have everything. She took a long, cooling drink of her shandy. It was the equivalent of counting ten before she said: 'Did Nick Brookes really phone you just to tittle-tattle about me?'

Paul examined the head on his beer. 'No. Some time ago I just happened to mention to him in passing that the life-style of lodging with Mrs Taylor was driving me to drink. I asked him to keep his eyes open and tip me the wink if he heard of a likely property coming on the market.'

'And he rang to tell you he'd heard of something suitable?' Eve said hopefully. Because anything, even his own cooking, would surely be preferable to Mrs Taylor's burnt offerings.

'That's about the long and short of it.'

She clicked her tongue. Why were men so teasingly unforthcoming? Another woman would have spilled out all the meaty details without her having to ask: 'And is it?'

Even more infuriating still, he said: 'Is it what?'

'Is the property suitable?'

'Tell you better tomorrow evening. I've a permit to view straight after school tomorrow.' A look in his eye told her he considered he'd teased her long enough, and to her considerable satisfaction he added: 'Why not come with me? I could use the feminine viewpoint.'

What was more, she knew it wasn't a spur of the moment invitation; it gave her a warmly satisfying feeling to know he'd intended asking her to accompany him all along. 'Tell you what, we'll make a night of it. Have a meal somewhere. What do you say?'

She accepted: 'Lovely.' Considered what to wear. Unless she wanted to be ribbed all day about her unusually elegant appearance, she'd have to take a change of clothes with her to slip into after school.

Paul finished his beer, saw that Eve was only really a good sip into her shandy, took his empty tankard and the plate containing the unappetising remains of his meat pie to the bar counter, and returned with a half.

'Now then,' he said, settling himself low in his seat for a good listening session. 'Tell me how you made out with your cousin. Shelley Anne, isn't it?'

In keeping with most women, Eve liked nothing better than having a tale to tell and a receptive audience to tell it to. Funny thing was, there wasn't a lot she wanted to tell Paul about Shelley Anne.

'Guess who drove us from the station?' she said. Yes, that was neutral enough. 'The artist, Peregrine Anthony Adamson, who's rented old Lettie Lomas's cottage.'

'Don't tell me the mystery man has shown up at last? I was beginning to think he was a figment of the property agent's imagination.'

'Apparently he rented the cottage, dumped his stuff and then had to go back to London on a spot of unfinished business.'

'You must be one of the few people to meet him.'

On their way home, Eve and Paul had to pass the cottage with the yellow door. The curtains weren't drawn to, and a flicker of firelight dwelt on the oak ceiling beams and gave the room a cosy glow. The cottage seemed to have died when Lettie Lomas, something of a local character, big on folk-lore, and locally well-loved, was buried in the churchyard cemetary. It was nice to see the cottage coming to life, and Eve was just about to comment on its lived-in glow, when Paul's arm shaped to her waist. Not amorously, although her heart leapt responsively as his fingers dug into her side, but drawing her attention to something inside the cottage.

At first, all Eve could see was the dark outline Tony made. Very gently, Paul eased Eve in front of him, and from this slightly different angle she could see the tall, slim figure of a girl pressed close in Tony's arms. It was not possible to see who the girl was. In the firelight glow they were just a hump, scarcely recognisable as two people.

The utter stillness and melting softness of the girl's body outlined her total dedication and lack of resistance, her pure and utter enjoyment.

It must be quite something, thought Eve, to let a man hold you like that and dare to submit so totally to him.

You wouldn't have to care, or hope his head was cool enough to put on the brake. She knew she would never forget that moment of seeing Tony and his unknown conquest.

She felt Paul's fingers aching into her side. Something about Tony and the girl struck a chord of envy; a warm and mysterious stirring started up inside of her, making her feel quite weak. She yearned for that tight, breath-denying, body crushing embrace. She knew that when she reached her own front door, if Paul took her in his arms for a goodnight kiss, her lips would not hold back. She could feel them moist against her teeth, throbbing and fiercely giving.

Paul said, as they continued walking up the street, 'One of the few, perhaps, but definitely not the only one who knows our mystery artist, Peregrine Anthony, whatever you said his name was.'

'He likes to be called Tony. Tony Adamson.'

'Not taking his earlier flying visit into account, Tony Adamson has been in Hawsbury for less than half a day. Unless he brought her with him, we must assume he's a quick worker.'

'He didn't bring anybody with him to my knowledge. He was alone when Shelley Anne and I enlisted his help at the station.'

'You?' The helpless female act didn't fit Eve.

'Well — ' She laughed — 'Mainly Shelley Anne.'

'Quick worker then,' mused Paul. 'Mighty quick worker, I'd say. A man could know a girl half a lifetime, and not know her that well.'

So he'd seen it too, that putty in the hands responsiveness; seen it and was perhaps contrasting it with her marked holding back that time he'd taken her in his arms. Oddly enough, that had happened after a visit to the Elephant and Castle. If she had held herself at arm's length, it was because of her mood, and not through lack of desire. It was the day Shelley Anne's letter arrived asking if she could come to stay; enough to put any girl with less going for her out of humour. And now Shelley Anne was here, and instead of the looks-gap closing, it had widened. Way across the chasm of mere prettiness, Shelley Anne was ravishingly beautiful.

But Eve didn't care how many heads Shelley Anne might turn, so long as Paul's eyes didn't swerve in her direction. Away you go, Shelley Anne. I'm banishing you from my thoughts. You're not going to spoil this moment for me.

Their steps slowed automatically as they reached Eve's door. Eve didn't know whether to bless or curse the fact that privacy was a poor illusion cast by the shadow of the house. She knew she was going to let Paul worry about the proprieties. Let him consider his position as headmaster in the town; let him take into account the limits set by the public nature of the venue and the standard of behaviour the townspeople would find acceptable. She wasn't going to hold back on one warm look, that was for sure.

But had it been a one-way hesitancy? Hadn't she felt it in her bones that Paul was as tied up inside himself as she was? Had Paul just wanted amorous contact and free use of her kisses, he would have made sure they walked a more private path. It was as if he'd deliberately kept it in the public eye until deeper instincts were satisfied. Perhaps Eve wasn't the only one to want at least a hint of a declaration; perhaps he needed some sign from her before he could step over his own caution and reach out for her.

There was in Paul a streak of self-effacement. Was he unsure of himself, less arrogant in love than he might have been because once he'd been too sure and come unstuck? At the back of Eve's mind there was always the shadowy figure of the girl she suspected of being on his.

There might have been such a girl once — but she was not with him now. Shadows dramatised his face, but there was no bitter veil of memory paining his eyes, only a look in them that made her lower hers.

Her breath scalded her throat, her heart leapt crazily. 'Paul . . . ' Her voice was an ache, a plea, an assurance.

And then it happened. The unbelievable. And out of a sweetly benign sky at that. Or had they been too engrossed in each other to notice the clouds banking in menacing black thunderheads? It was such a sensitive moment that it shouldn't have rained. The rain was practically a recrimination as it teamed down on them.

'I thought I might have to keep a weather eye open for the likes of Miss Meakin,' said Paul, referring to their kill-joy, prudish fellow teacher. 'But this is certainly one in the eye for my ardour that I didn't expect.' He grinned, casting humour on the situation. 'There's nothing as dampening as rain.'

So it was that he didn't kiss her warm, amorous lips, but her laughing lips. Then, placing his hand on her back, he pushed her inside her own front door. She leaned against the door, the concave hollow of her spine tingling as though his fingers still rested there, listening to the effect distance had of softening his footsteps as he continued up the street to his lodgings. No Rubicon had been crossed this night, no decisive, irrevocable step taken, and yet Eve had the feeling that she and Paul had managed to get on a warmer footing.

'Hi!' she said, pushing open the living room door. But there was only her father there to say:'Oh, there you are, Eve. It's started to rain then?'

'Just,' she said, thinking, 'Mean weather!' and suppressing the laughter bubbling sweetly in her throat. 'Where's Mother?'

'She thought she'd have an early night.'

'Isn't she well?' Quick concern flooded Eve's eyes.

'Just a headache.'

'Shall I make cocoa all round?'

'Make two cups for now. You and I can have a natter over them. We don't often have the opportunity to talk. And then you can make two more cups for your mother and Shelley Anne and take them up with you as you go to bed.'

'You're on,' said Eve.

He picked up the newspaper he'd been reading, and Eve went through to the kitchen. She sang under her breath as she made the cocoa, although she wasn't conscious of the fact.

William Masters wished he could attribute his daughter's cheerfulness to her having come to terms with her cousin's visit. But his keen ears had picked up the footsteps continuing up the street after Eve had come into the house.

'Bump into anyone interesting while

you were out?' he called through the open door.

Drink-making activities halted, Eve's face was plastered with a cheeky grin as she poked it round the door. 'Only Paul,' she said. Then whisked back out of sight.

Eve brought in the two mugs of cocoa. Set her father's cocoa on the table at his side, and went to sit across from him in the chair, bending to put her mug down on the floor and to unlace her shoes before kicking them off. She picked up the mug and without spilling a drop, altered her position until she was sitting with her legs curled under her.

'Well, Dad,' she said. It wasn't a question, just a companionable sound.

'Well, lass,' he said.

Eve wondered if her father knew how much more she'd appreciated him since his illness. One should know a person's worth, but it's human nature not to.

A relaxing talk and half an hour later, Eve carried two mugs of cocoa upstairs. Her mother's sleepy grunt told her to leave one mug on the bedside table, and: 'Thank you, dear.'

Then Eve climbed the stairs to Shelley Anne's quarters. A pencil beam of light showed under the door.

'Come in,' said Shelley Anne in answer to her knock.

'I thought you might like a bedtime drink.'

'Cocoa?' said Shelley Anne. Her tone of voice said, 'How quaint!'

'It seemed a good idea at the time. Throw it down the sink if you don't want it.' Eve didn't mean to sound brusque; she was reacting to what her cousin's manner was giving out.

Shelley Anne said: 'Don't be cross with me, Eve. If I don't know how to accept ordinary acts of caring, it's because none has been shown to me for such a long time.'

Perhaps if Shelley Anne had told Eve what was in her heart at that moment, the cousins would have reached that desired area of friendship and understanding. If Shelley Anne had said, 'Help me, Eve.' If she could have stripped the guarding humour from her eyes and let Eve see the encircling hurt and pain, through to the dangerous areas of sobbing self-pity, her tender-hearted cousin would have been the first to want to help her on the road to recovery.

But Shelley Anne had dwelt so long in lies that she'd forgotten the value of the simple truth. The truth was a trap, never an ally. She turned from it, snuffing out the weeping, aching need, and hid behind the false dazzle of her brightest and most mocking smile.

Raising the unwanted mug of cocoa to her lips, she said: 'Let's see if it tastes as revolting as it looks.'

The rain pattered down on the roof, and for no reason that Eve could think of, contrition bit at her throat.

'Have you been out?' she said, because she couldn't think of anything else to say.

Shelley Anne's chin lifted defiantly. 'No.'

'But . . . '

Eve knew why, of all the subjects she could have picked on, she'd chosen that particular one. Shelley Anne's hair was rain-spangled. Not only had she been out, she'd only just come in. If Eve had come straight upstairs with the cocoa, instead of making two batches and stopping to talk to her father, she didn't think she would have caught Shelley Anne in.

It wasn't as if she was prying, she had just been trying to make compatible conversation, and she couldn't see the point of Shelley Anne's silly lie. It wasn't as if Shelley Anne knew anybody in Hawsbury, so she couldn't have gone out on a secret assignation. Obviously she'd felt the need for a breath of air, and so she'd slipped out quietly using the outside stairs. It was a silly, pointless lie. As pointless as Shelley Anne's lie to Tony at the railway station.

But why should she worry about Shelley Anne's inability to tell the simple truth.

'Good night,' she said, a circle of ice ringing her mouth.

5

Next morning, Eve got up earlier than usual. She used the extra time to decide on an outfit suitable for viewing a property with Paul, one which would happily go along to wherever Paul planned to take her for a meal.

It would have to be something that didn't get into tucks at the sight of a carrier bag. It had to be taken with her this morning and stored at school all day because it was her week for dinner duty. The dress that embodied both attractiveness and uncrushability was a fairly new acquisition to her wardrobe, which meant that Paul hadn't seen it. It was a singing out, sunshiny sort of dress. As yellow and as unsophisticated as butter, it had the advantage of spinning a girl into golden delight. The colour alone would win an Olympic medal for reaching dizzy heights of happiness. Add that to a fit which gave Eve a waist that was infinitesimal, while clinging fetchingly to create an opposite illusion elsewhere. As Eve didn't have the sort of measurements that nobly filled a sweater, she was pleased with this effect.

It needed something, a pendant with a topaz drop or a brooch in gold filigree work to set it off.

Her friend, Avril Speight, sold jewellery in her curio shop. On impulse, Eve set off for school earlier to give herself time to call in and see Avril on the offchance she could produce something suitable.

In height, Avril matched up to Shelley Anne. Although Avril didn't have anything like Shelley Anne's claim to beauty, she did have flame-red hair and enough style to pull the wool over a lot of eyes. Today, the wool, in an unlikely combination of caramel and Beaujolais stripes, had been knitted in a simple rib pattern on giant-sized needles. Eve felt that if she'd tried it, it would have looked like a dish cloth.

Round, and that is the key word; Avril's magnificent bosom, and matched with clotted cream pants, it looked Paris couture. Or French revolution. Eve couldn't quite make her mind up which. When she'd finished telling Avril how fabulous she thought she looked, Eve explained her mission.

'How do you look in the dress?' Avril asked practically.

Eve thought for a moment. 'Like a golden rose,' she answered immodestly.

Avril smiled, and then went to a show case. She came back holding something in the palm of her hand. She held out her hand, uncurled her fingers in a movement so graceful that it gave the impression of a flower opening its petals, and said: 'Appropriate, don't you think?'

In Avril's outstretched palm lay a gold brooch fashioned in the shape of a rose. Its beauty glistened Eve's eyes. She squinted covetously at the price tag. It didn't carry the retail price, but she knew Avril's cost code because she sometimes helped Avril out in the shop on busy Saturdays. She concentrated on the letters, worked it out in her mind, and blinked.

'It is nine carat gold,' said Avril in a soft, apologetic kind of voice.

'I'm not saying it's not worth it,' said Eve.

'You don't have to add the profit percentage to that,' said Avril, pointing to the code lettering.

The spark of hope extinguished as quickly as it had come to Eve's eye. 'That's a loony way to run a business. I couldn't.'

'Actually, you'd be doing me a favour. I fell in love with it and bought it in a weak moment. I won't be able to sell it. It's far too expensive for round here.'

Regretfully Eve shook her head. 'I'm not fooled, Avril. I know you're being generous, but even so I can't manage it. I'm only just recovering from the price I paid for the dress.

'Oh well, you can't say I didn't try,'

said Avril, going back to the showcase, lifting up the glass door and sliding the brooch back on its pad of black velvet.

'Shouldn't that be locked,' said Eve, noting the omission.

'It should be, but I've lost the key. I'll get a new key made eventually, but there's no hurry. Nobody's going to pinch anything here. Now, let me see if I've anything else suitable for your dress. Ah yes! I think I know what will do the trick.' And Avril produced the type of gold-effect filigree brooch Eve had had in mind in the first place. Not as pretty as the gold rose, but then nothing could be, and this didn't give her purse indigestion.

There followed one of those days so harrowing that Eve wondered by what conceit she'd imagined she had the patience to be a schoolteacher. Charlotte Brookes, the most intelligent child in the class, was playing her up by acting like the dullest. If Kevin Baxter nodded his head much more he'd nod right off to sleep. Doubtless he'd been up before five this morning to attend to his paper round. And as last night had been late night shopping at the supermarket where he worked, he would have been lucky to see his bed before eleven. Automatically, Eve searched the class for the other child who tugged at her heart-strings. But chirpy little Cheryl Carter wasn't present, for the third time that week! The note she'd bring would say Cheryl had either had a billious attack or been under the weather with a bad cold. Whereas Eve knew full well that Cheryl had been purposely kept home to cook lunch for her mother and father, two brothers and a sister.

Cheryl turned up for the afternoon session, bringing with her the anticipated note. It made Eve's blood boil, but there was nothing she could do about it, except to plough on and try to follow Alice Meakin's practise of not getting too intense about situations that could not be bettered. The senior teacher had a point when she said, 'Look, if it would help matters I'd bang my head against the wall. But it wouldn't help the children and all I'd achieve is a headache.'

'Miss,' a distressed voice piped up from the back row. 'Somebody's nicked my bus fare.'

'Are you quite sure, Amanda. You didn't spend the money at lunchtime and you aren't just saying this to get yourself out of a fix?'

'No, Miss — ' Eyes enlarging and brightening to a point just short of tears. 'I wouldn't do a thing like that Miss. I left the money in my desk and now it's gone.'

'Well just make sure it's not hiding under anything, a text book for example. If it's really gone, come to me after the lesson and I'll make up the loss.' Her eyes raked the faces of her class. 'Stealing is one thing I will not tolerate. If I catch the culprit he, or she, will be dealt with most severely.' Nobody paled or noticeably quaked in their seats. Sometimes Eve wondered if these distractions weren't a put-up job. There were certainly enough of them.

Barely had she said: 'We'll resume the lesson now,' than the bell rang to mark home-time.

She had tucked a spare coat-hanger in the carrier bag with her yellow dress and it hung behind the door of the staff room like a yellow smile. The staff room incorporated facilities for washing.

Alice Meakin entered the room, a look of pleased hesitancy on her face at sight of Eve. This surprised Eve. She was more often the recipient of Alice Meakin's disapproval.

'Ah . . . you haven't gone, Eve. I'd hoped . . . I wanted to talk to you.' A faded eye turned to view the dress. 'Yours? I once had a yellow dress similar to this one. Only mine had little bows on the sleeves, here and here. Are you going out? Straight from school?'

'Yes, I am.'

'Are you in a dreadful hurry? Have you time to talk to me first? There's something I must tell someone. I'd like it to be you. But if you haven't time . . . ?'

I haven't the time, Miss Meakin Neither have I the inclination for that matter. My day hasn't been too good. I don't teach children, I teach half-wits. Correction. I teach little fiends, tormenting horrors. I want to make up my face and tidy my hair; I want to put on my beautiful yellow dress and hurry to meet Paul. I can't wash my hands of this school day soon enough.

But there was an expression on Alice Meakin's face that made Eve blank out what was on hers, so that Alice Meakin and whatever odd thing she wanted to discuss with Eve, was the only reality.

Eve sat down, folded her hands in a pose of tranquillity and said: 'Of course I've time to listen. All the time in the world.'

'That's very kind of you. But then, basically, you are a very kind person.

You're naturally tolerant of another's failings. Not that I am . . . failing.' She looked down at her untinted finger-nails. 'I did see him. I saw my Bert.'

Eve waited patiently.

Alice Meakin continued: 'Not my Bert as he was then. But as he would be now, if he'd got through the war and lived. They said he was dead, but I never believed them. Don't you see, it means I've been right all these years, and that by some miracle he managed to survive.'

'Where did you think you saw him?'

'Not *think*, Eve. I saw him come out of the churchyard, large as life. His hair was grey, whereas it used to be jet black, and he didn't seem as tall as I remembered him, but that's probably because he's thickened out. When I got over the shock, I ran up the street after him. I assumed he'd cut through the churchyard to get to the car park. But I'd hesitated too long, and he'd gone.'

'Gone?'

Eve was thinking that people don't just vanish.

As if divining her thoughts, Miss Meakin replied: 'Not into thin air. Just gone. Perhaps he wasn't making for the car park. There was a bus coming, he could have hopped on that, or gone down any of the side streets. I looked down various streets, but I couldn't see anything of him. I daren't make a prolonged search, because it would have made me late back for school. I bumped into Charlotte Brookes' stepmother. The last person I'd choose as a confidante, but I had to tell someone and she was on the spot.'

'So you told Lilith Brookes?'

'With disastrous consequence. She didn't say anything, but I could tell by the way she sneered that she thought I was ready to be locked up in an institute.'

'If it's just Lilith Brookes' opinion that's bothering you . . . ?'

'Not bothering me, exactly, but

116

causing me a little unease. Nicholas Brookes has a finger in most local affairs. He'd only have to think I wasn't suitable to teach the youth of Hawsbury for me to be out of a job.'

'Why should Lilith Brookes want to stir up something like that? It's lunatic.' Eve would have called that opinion back if it had been within her power to do so.

But instead of taking offence, Alice Meakin's tight expression relaxed into the makings of a smile. 'Yes it is, isn't it?' And the awakened smile-lines fanned out into relief. 'That's what I've been telling myself. I had to hear it from someone else's lips. Seeing my Bert again, after all this time, had made me feel overwrought. Upset my reasoning power. Thank you so much for listening to me. I'll be off now, and let you pretty yourself up in peace. Have a nice time.'

'Thank you, Miss Meakin, I'll certainly do my best. Miss Meakin?'

'Yes?'

But in all kindness Eve couldn't say, 'You're more overwrought than you think. Go home and put your feet up and rest. Let that old dragon of a mother you live with look after you for a change.' She couldn't say she thought Alice Meakin was sane in one breath and advise her to take it easy the next. Poor Miss Meakin, she thought. People don't come back from the dead.

* * *

'Just . . . goodnight,' she said lamely.

Sighing softly to herself, she went to get ready for Paul. She came out of the staff room to find Paul stationed at the door. He had the appearance of a man who's been waiting so long that his patience is beginning to peel off in strips.

'And high time too,' was all he said.

Despite the minutes that had been shaved off her getting-ready time, Eve was more than satisfied with her appearance. But the confirmation in Paul's eyes was appreciated just the same.

'I'm sorry to keep you waiting. Alice Meakin waylaid me. I just had to stay and listen to her.'

'Don't apologise, Eve, for being there when somebody needed you.'

How could he know that? What had she said that told him everything wasn't as it should be with Miss Meakin? She felt ashamed that she'd not been more vigilant in guarding the trust put in her. She hadn't meant to break faith. Oh, she hadn't told Paul anything really, she'd just forgotten how quick he was at assessing situations. From now on, he'd be watching Miss Meakin for signs.

'Go on,' he prompted.

'I think we both know I've said more than I intended already.'

His expression, still quietly pursuing, veered toward a smile. 'Very predictable.'

Her chin shot up. 'Are you laughing at me?'

'Would I? Loyalty is an admirable quality. Too bad there's not more of it around.'

'Sorry. It's just that I'm prickly because I feel that I've been disloyal.'

'Will it help if I tell you it's nothing you've said?'

He took hold of her fingers, tugging them until she brought her eyes up to look at him. He held her glance by sheer force of will, even after he'd spoken and it would have suited her to look away.

What he said to disconcert her was: 'Isn't it about time you realised you can trust me?'

It was on the tip of Eve's tongue to say, 'But I do trust you.' It remained unsaid, because it wasn't true. You couldn't trust someone completely, and hold back during the intimate holding-close moments; if you trusted a person you accepted them for what they were, and didn't spend half your time puzzling about why they didn't fit into the mould they'd cast round themselves. You didn't continually question it and pain to chip at it until you'd exposed a chink of what lay underneath.

Although she was looking through chimeric eyes, she knew she wouldn't find a serpent's head on a goat's body. But at the same time she had more than a hint of an idea that she wouldn't find solid schoolmaster material all the way through. Paul Smalley had an interesting side kick to him.

As if to demonstrate that, he took her by the shoulders and kissed her. His lips pressed hers, then gently enfolded her mouth. It had the beginnings of a passionate kiss, even if the school surroundings forbad it the depths.

She felt a slow, sweet unwinding inside. She felt safe and trusting.

Paul teased: 'One day we'll synchronise this climate of feeling with the privacy of more suitable surroundings. And then look out. If you give me just half this encouragement, I'll not be responsible for the consequences. What do you say to that, Miss Masters?'

'Nothing to say to that, Mr Smalley.' Letting her eyelashes glide down.

He gave a little grunt, and then he said: 'We've a house to view on the other side of the moor at Ayskirk.' He pulled her arm through his and marched her down the corridor.

'So far? Isn't Ayskirk where Nicholas Brookes lives? So if you buy the property, you'll be neighbours.'

'Huh-uh.'

He waited until they were seated in his car and the wheel was lively beneath his fingers before he threw at her. 'Will it spoil your pleasure if I tell you that after we've looked at the property and had a bite to eat somewhere, I promised Nick we'd look in for a drink?'

'Oh Paul, not that? You couldn't have! I don't fit in. Lilith Brookes looks at me as if I've crawled from under a stone.'

There was a light salting of mischief in the glance Paul swung across at her.

'Stop being catty about Lilith. I can't think why you've got it in for her.'

Swallowing on the unpalatable truth of that, Eve said: 'It's funny you should say that, because for a long time I couldn't think why either. Then it suddenly came to me that what I feel is reaction. Lilith Brookes doesn't like me.'

'Why not?'

'How should I know? Have you known Nicholas Brookes a long time?'

'Long enough to have played in the same rugby scrum. Well enough to have courted the same girl and still remain friends. It's a good friendship, despite the fact we don't see eye to eye about a lot of things. Nick will certainly never be an extension of my mind. It's remarkable, really, how well we get on together. We grew up in the same town. Lilith, too, for that matter. If Nick hadn't thought to contact me when the headship at Grange Lane became vacant; *we* wouldn't have met. Surely that's worth something, so be an angel and don't put up any silly objections. Anyway, I've already given my promise.'

'For yourself, so you go. You can't promise for someone else.'

Eve knew she was giving the matter an importance that was disproportionate. She was stinging, and the horrible part was, she didn't know why. She was even glad when Paul knuckled her anger with gentle amusement.

'But you're not someone else. You're you. And I happen to want you with me.'

It would be daylight for hours yet, but as they crossed the moor in Paul's car, the light seemed to become softly diffused. Not quite an eerie glow, but . . .

It was a new feeling and one Eve didn't particularly like. She didn't have a taste for precognition. She'd romped every inch of this moor and found it a golden playground, even in obliterating rain or murky half-light, so why had it suddenly taken on this unrecognisable face of foreboding?

If she'd believed in the supernatural, she would have accredited this feeling of flesh tightening on bones to some sort of preternatural warning. It was sparkling daylight, yet the moor was fretted with a dark and evil omniscience. The darkness was the scaffolding of some event. Was it in the safe past and had time not troubled to remove the framework of a plan that had already taken place? Or was it in the future, waiting in the wings of time for its cue to happen?

Paul's voice was sharply astringent, and as reviving as a sniff of smelling-salts. 'If the thought of going to the Brookes' makes you go white about the gills, then forget it. We won't go.'

'No, it's not that. Such a funny feeling came over me. Like a . . . premonition of something.'

'Whatever it was, it's shaken you up. It might be as well to give Nick's a miss.'

What a lovely get-out. Was she a

fool not to grab it?

'Honestly Paul, it was just a moment's indisposition. I feel fine now.'

And that was the truth. If Paul hadn't been with her to bear witness to her loss of colour, she would have thought she'd imagined it. But something had made her feel queasy.

She wound down the window a few inches and the wind blew in sweetly from over the moor that was once again her golden playground. And it was as if she'd never felt that skin-crawling moment of unease.

6

In life one get's flashes of perception. Without appreciating how or why, Eve knew that Paul's househunting quest would not find success today.

No sign of the house yet, but the approach was everything one dreamed of. A stream ran down the main street, and on either side lurched old cottages with lichen-covered, lime-stone walls, arched doorways and mullioned windows. They had a funny, yet lovingly preserved, lop-sided appearance. It was the sort of idyllic setting that attracts one's peace-loving instincts.

During the summer months, tourists would drive through on their way to a more publicised spot, slowing perhaps to snap a brief sunshine memory. But for the most part, Ayskirk was still a slumbrous beauty spot that had not yet been harshly jerked awake by the kiss of the twentieth century motorised man.

The house they had come to see was climbing out of the village. Although of a more recent vintage than the cottages, local materials had been used so that its mellow facade merged with the surroundings.

The previous owner had left the curtains up at the windows to give it an air of occupancy, but it still had a blank and shuttered look about it. Eve had once heard a solitary type of person spoken of as having a lonely look at the back of the eyes. Substitute windows for eyes and the description could fit the house. The only wrong note was the car parked in the drive.

Paul swung through the gates and pulled up smoothly behind it.

'Whose can that be?' he puzzled, getting out. His expression was a give-away. He was already considering the possibility that somebody had pipped him at the post.

He strode on ahead, as if impatient to learn the unpleasant truth. Following close behind, Eve consoled herself with the thought that it looked too expensive for Paul to afford anyway. So it was she entered the front door to the sound of Paul greeting someone he obviously knew.

'Good evening, Mr. Rowland. What are you doing here?'

The reply came wafting to Eve on the distinctive smell of pipe tobacco. 'Same as you, lad. Only I've been a bit sharper off the mark.'

'What do you mean?'

'Pretty much what you think I mean. The deal has been closed most satisfactorily and the agent has just this minute gone. Sorry and all that.'

'I should think so.'

By this time Eve had caught up. She took a tentative step from the hall with its magically romantic twist of staircase, into a large room with a stone fireplace pacing the length of one wall. All this she gleaned from the corner of her eye; she was more interested in assessing Paul's expression which was slipping from would-you-believe-it annoyance into wry humour. Then the very words that had sprung into Eve's head leapt from Paul's mouth. 'Would you believe it, but this cheeky blighter has bought my house!'

'Not your house, Paul,' stressed Eve.

'It would have been if I hadn't told him about it. Next time I'll keep my mouth shut until the contract's in my pocket.

Eve thought Paul was taking it in good humour. She agreed wholeheartedly when Paul's grey-haired friend said: 'I'll say this, lad, you're a good loser.' And then he added ambiguously, 'But then, you always were. Now introduce me to the little lady. And should I thank her for delaying you long enough to allow me to pull it off?'

'You should,' Paul said drily, while Eve squirmed, very delicately. 'Mr Rowland, I'd like you to meet a good friend of mine who is also a teacher. Eve Masters — Hubert Rowland. Mr Rowland comes from

130

my home town, Eve.'

Eve was surprised to find her hand in a hard, calloused grip. This house hadn't conditioned her to expect a working hand. She realised, to her acute embarrassment, how accurately Hubert Rowland was reading her thoughts when she saw the awakening network of deep and much used laughter lines around his mouth. His fine tan hadn't been acquired on a holiday beach as she'd first thought, but was the result of long days spent out of doors in the course of his work. In his mid fifties, he had the build and thickset shoulders of a farmer or a bricklayer; and a little fun demon lived permanently in his top pocket, just waiting for moments such as this to leap into his eye.

'The manner in which Eve was delayed makes the joke even more delicious than you think, my friend,' Paul told Hubert Rowland to Eve's further confusion.

They were like two small boys sharing a joke. It explained nothing to Eve to hear Paul say: 'I was left cooling my heels in the corridor while Eve was gossiping with a fellow teacher.' But an alert look crossed Hubert Rowland's face, as if a message had been passed to him.

He gave a brief, understanding nod which obviously closed the subject, because then he turned to Eve and said: 'You work at Paul's school.'

It was a statement that wasn't a question and yet still required an affirmative: 'Yes, I do.'

'What's on the agenda for you two now?' said Hubert Rowland, managing to address the remark to Paul while sending Eve his slow sweet smile. She liked him. She liked his sauce. She minused thirty years from his age; he would have been a charmer in his day.

'Drive out somewhere for a meal,' Paul was explaining. 'And then track back to Nick's because I promised we'd look in for a drink later.' Of course, as they all originated from the same town, Hubert Rowland would be acquainted with Nick, and Lilith too for that matter.

Hubert Rowland mused genially: 'I wonder, seeing as I've bought your house as it were, would you let me buy you two bright young things your dinner?'

Eve's eyes were there, waiting to waylay Paul's. As kind as the invitation was, and much as she liked Hubert Rowland, she wanted to spend the next hour alone with Paul. She needed that as compensation for having to accompany him to the off-putting Brookes' house. And anyway she couldn't really believe Hubert Rowland wanted them to accept. He just felt it necessary to make the gesture because of the trick he'd pulled on Paul. And then, just as she was beginning to despair of making contact, Paul's eyes met hers, but his got in the first signal and it was a plea for understanding.

'That's very kind of you, Mr Rowland. We'd be delighted to accept. Although,

I'll give you due warning, I feel very strongly about the house and I intend to retaliate by ordering the most expensive item on the menu.'

As soon as Paul got to the accept bit, Hubert Rowland's face lit up. Eve remembered her substitute observation about the house. A lonely look at the back of its windows. Said in the original context: eyes for windows, it would fit the man. Because of his gregarious personality, she had failed to see the lonely look at the back of his eyes.

As it was Hubert Rowland's show, Paul amiably agreed to leave his car for collection later. They all piled into Hubert Rowland's car in search of a likely place to eat. It meant that Paul did not have the opportunity of explaining his action to Eve, or of thanking her for accepting the change of plan without fuss. Eve had a vague but warm feeling that his eyes were doing the job for him.

Although still not dark, the sky was

preparing its soft journey into night. Hubert Rowland tossed in Eden Hall Restaurant as a possible place to eat. Without doubt this was the most high-priced place within easy driving distance and Eve fully expected Paul to demur on that account. She didn't think Paul would allow Hubert Rowland to go to that expense.

To her surprise, Paul said affably: 'You're paying the piper and to my ear that's a very nice tune. Does it suit you, Eve?'

'It was Eve I was thinking about when I made the suggestion,' said Hubert Rowland. 'Eden seemed very appropriate.'

The meal was a more leisurely affair than Paul had planned. The chef had maintained his usual high standard. Eating at Eden Hall, with its atmosphere of past grandeur preserved, proving its quality by slipping untarnished into this century, was always a pleasant and luxurious entertainment.

For Eve's part, she felt the chef

had surpassed even his own skill and ingenuity this time. After a chicken dish in a rich piquant sauce she had declared she couldn't eat another thing. But when the sweets trolley arrived, her eyes turned into goblets drinking in the varied and exciting looking concoctions, and she'd been torn with childlike indecision which to choose. The final choice was narrowed down to two: a lush chocolate gateau, and a meringue swan sailing on cherries in wine. To her shame, and the menfolk's delight, she needed very little persuasion to have both.

They retired to the lounge; Eve, and Hubert Rowland sank into deep armchairs to await the arrival of the coffee. Paul excused himself to telephone Nicholas Brookes to explain that he and Eve would be arriving later than anticipated.

Hubert Rowland watched Eve's eyes as they followed Paul's straight back. It was obvious that Paul had told her very little about himself. The mention that they both came from the same town had filled her eyes with questions. About Nick and Lilith. And relationships . . . those which alter as affections change, and those which are as deep and unalterable as the blood that runs in our veins.

Because Paul wasn't there to see, Eve's guard was relaxed and the wonder and whirlpool of her emotions was reflected as a lovely thing to see in her eyes.

Hubert Rowland's lids narrowed in pain-touched memory. He had seen just this look, perhaps wider and even more gullible, in a young and lovely girl's eyes many years ago. He had been the recipient of just such a tender love, and he couldn't look the truth in the face if he didn't admit to himself that it had been that last remembered look that kept him going through the grim years. The shining promise in their depths had been the lifeline he'd clung to during the hideous days and nights of black torment. I promise my undying love, the look had said.

Circumstance had been the black serpent making it impossible for him to come back and claim that love. Seeing that same trusting look now in Eve's eyes made him want to lean forward and say, 'Beware . . . there's a serpent in every garden.' But even forewarned, what could she do? Everyone knows about the serpent. It doesn't have to be an outside force; sometimes it's in oneself in the form of jealousy or a hasty tongue. The trick is to recognise what form your particular serpent has taken, and there arises the difficulty. Such discernment prefers a mellower companion. It and youth do not walk easily together.

The coffee arrived. And so did Paul.

'I got through, eventually. I told Nick to expect us in half an hour. Nick said why don't you come with us,' Paul told Hubert Rowland. 'Why don't you? You know as well as I do, it will be all right.'

'You know as well as I do,' said

with full meaning, and not a flowery preface. Or was she being imaginative again, Eve wondered.

'No, I've no intention of foisting myself on you any more this evening.'

Eve's mouth rushed open to say: 'It wouldn't be that. We've enjoyed your company, haven't we Paul?'

'In that case,' said Hubert Rowland, taking out his pipe, lighting it at third attempt and puffing contentedly, 'we must do this again. Yes . . . and we won't be too long about it either. This doesn't bother you, does it?' — indicating his pipe.

It was later, and Eve was alone with Paul in his car, and they were on their way to Nicholas Brookes' house. It was necessary to skirt a narrow section of the moor again, but this time Eve felt no prickly sensation of unease. The phantoms had gone, even though it was the hour when shadows huddle. Grey gelatinous shapes joining and leaping apart in the final romp before the day was entirely spent. Already the darkness was thickening. It was that interim period of murky blackness before the moon has properly risen.

It was a short journey, a few minutes at the most from the house, which was now Hubert Rowland's house, to where Nicholas Brookes lived.

Eve said: 'I'm sorry you didn't get your house, Paul.'

Realising there would be no time to talk about it later, and wanting to say what had to be said and done with it, Paul stopped the car short of the Brookes' house. 'I'm sorry I didn't get the house too, Eve. But I'll tell you this, I couldn't have lost it to a nicer bloke.'

'I realised that. He's a very sincere person.'

'And a lonely one.'

'I gathered that as well.'

'He had a dual purpose in looking me up. The old friend angle and . . . well he wanted a first-hand report on someone I know, who happens to be someone he knew a long time ago.

It's all a bit sad really. I couldn't have run out him tonight no matter what we'd planned.'

'I realised that but . . . ' How could she ask if Hubert Rowland could afford Eden Hall prices without slighting Paul? Paul wasn't a take-on. He was obviously content on that score and that should be enough for her.

'Hubert Rowland hasn't had too good a life. He was a P.O.W. in the last lot. But before that he got involved with a girl. I don't think he intended letting it get as serious as it did. On his part it was a bit of fun, although he was perfectly aware that she'd fallen like a ton of bricks for him. They say this is the permissive age, but I think it was the war years that put the boot in a lot of people's notions of morality. I don't say it was a jot more right then than it is now, but at least they had the incentive to go off the rails. Eat, drink and be merry for tomorrow you may be blown into kingdom come. Food was on ration, drink at blackmarket prices and practically unobtainable, that didn't leave them much to rid their high spirits on. When Hubert Rowland told me about this, he didn't try to defend himself. He said openly that he hoped to seduce her for the price of an engagement ring, only he came unstuck. He fell in love with her.'

Eve shook her head in dazed exasperation. 'I don't get this double standard of morality. Why do girls have to fit into two categories: one to take liberties with, one to marry. And if Hubert Rowland changed his mind, why didn't he fit her into the other category? Why didn't he marry her?'

'Can't you guess? He was married already.'

'Ah, that would be a complication! So what happened then?'

'He took his time returning from his sally into enemy territory. He came back, via a prisoner of war camp, to Sophie, the girl he'd married at a ridiculously young age, during the early part of the war. Like a lot of other impetuous marriages of its time, theirs was a failure.'

'How tragic. Didn't he ever think of getting a divorce? I don't hold with divorce, but I think it's more honest than living with a person you can't love.'

'Perhaps. Who knows? He doesn't live with his wife now. Although there was never an official divorce, they separated ten years back.'

'And what about the other girl? His wartime sweetheart.'

'He tried to find her. The house she'd lived in was demolished by a stray bomb, probably intended for a nearby armaments factory. By the time Hubert Rowland arrived on the scene, all trace of rubble had been removed and all that was left was a gap where the house had been. He said he looked at the void and it brought it home to him how empty he felt inside. For his own peace of mind he knew he had to find her and see for himself that she was alive and well, even if he could never make himself known to her. He said he realised at that moment that it would be kinder to let her assume he'd perished in the war than have her know he'd deceived her. But tracking her down was easier said than done. He asked around, but most of the people were new to the street. Only one person remembered the family, an old man who'd no idea where they'd gone. And so, for a time, Hubert Rowland continued following false leads. Once he thought he'd caught up with her, but it turned out to be another girl of the same age with a similar name. It was as if Fate had taken a hand and wiped her clean off the face of the earth. So he got on with living his life. He patched things up with his wife and they even had a child, a daughter he dotes on. But he never forgot his wartime sweetheart. Odd thing is, once he stopped looking for her, he found her through the personal column of a daily newspaper. She was trying to trace him. He said he sat with the newspaper in his hand and cried like a boy. He said it comforted him to know where she was and that she was all right.'

'Grim comfort.'

'Yes.' His reply lacked that ring of finality. She felt her eyebrows sweeping up. 'Something else?'

'Recently, things have looked up for him financially. Looked up a lot. His wife has written to ask him for a reconciliation. And I'm not saying there's any connection between the two things. She wrote a lot of heart-tugging stuff about getting older and how silly it was for two people to live such lonely, separate lives.'

'Do you think it was in his mind to take his wife back when he went after the house?'

'I should say that was the last thing in his mind. If he'd planned to go back to his wife, he wouldn't deposit her less than twelve miles from his old sweetheart. The old passion must have dampened by now, but he must still think something about her, or why should he trouble to find out if she's well and happy.'

The time was ticking on. It wouldn't do to arrive too late at the Brookes'. A stickler for convention, Paul should be fretting to get there. Why had he reined his impatience to do something as out of character as passing on intimate details that must have been told to him in confidence? Why had he told her? Paul rarely acted without a motive. Why had he allowed her this peep into Hubert Rowland's very personal life?

It had certainly been a day for confidences. First Alice Meakin nabbing her to tell her about her Bert. Then Paul telling her about Hubert. It hit her just like that. Bert wasn't short for Albert as she'd thought, but Hubert. She knew why Paul had told her even if she hadn't worked all the implications out in her mind. And she knew Paul knew that she knew.

She heard his sharply drawn breath.

'I thought the penny was never going to drop.'

'Then Hubert's sweetheart is Alice Meakin?'

'Yes.'

'I wish you hadn't told me. You've put me in an absolutely impossible position.' She felt both fretful and resentful. 'Why did you tell me?'

'Hubert Rowland was in Hawsbury today. He says he got a little careless and he thinks Alice might have seen him.'

'She did. That's what she was telling me in the staff room. She was in such a state with herself that even though I knew I was going to make you late, I had to listen to her.'

'I was in the corridor when she came out of the staff room. Remember? After what Hubert Rowland told me, it wasn't difficult to guess what you'd been talking about. She had the look about her of someone who'd just unburdened.'

'Although she went out of her way

to deny it, she thinks her mind is playing tricks. She can't really believe her Bert has come back from the dead. For her own sanity I shall have to tell her.'

'You can't; irrespective of whether Hubert Rowland's right or wrong, I cannot betray his confidence.'

'You. Not me. I'm under no oath of secrecy. You should have considered that before you told me.'

'I told you because I had to. Alice Meakin has been behaving in a most peculiar way all afternoon. I knew it was because she'd had a shock. I wanted you to know that too. She needs a friend, Eve, and not one who secretly thinks she's gone off her rocker.'

'Yes but . . .'

'I'm not going to bind you either way. The situation could alter so that it might benefit Alice to know. I'm going to leave that to your sound common sense and integrity. At this particular moment, Hubert Rowland's own reasoning still makes the best sense.'

'What reasoning? I don't know what you mean.'

'Do you honestly think you'd be doing her a kindness by telling our most upright and honourable Miss Meakin the man she thought was coming back to marry her was a married man all the time? That he posed as a single man and gave her an engagement ring to . . .'

'You don't have to go on,' she hissed savagely. 'But she's middle aged now. Shouldn't she be given the opportunity to live the only life she's got to the full? She wouldn't be breaking up a marriage, because it's already broken up.'

'If you think Alice would even contemplate such a thing, you don't know her at all. She's too moral a person. Hubert Rowland knows that.'

'Does he? Deep down?' She didn't want to score off Paul, she just felt he wasn't getting the full picture.

'What do you mean?' Something about his tone was cross-graining her. He was too pleasantly patient.

'I think deep down he wants to be found out, otherwise he would have stayed put wherever he was living.'

'That doesn't necessarily follow. It is possible for people to live within this radius and never meet. It isn't Alice Meakin he's settling here to be near; but his daughter. Although perhaps he thinks he can kill two birds with one stone and keep an eye on his Alice, now he knows 'where she art.' '

'Oh, come on, Paul.' She was laughing at him because he couldn't really believe that. 'Is ever a man that quixotic? Could you love a woman and not ache to touch her? Think about it.'

He replied with mock solemnity: 'I've thought about it and it has disadvantages. Only *thinking* isn't a tenth as enjoyable.'

Instead of frowning, Eve felt her mouth more disposed to laughter. It came to her that she wasn't cross with Paul because he wasn't seeing the problem from exactly her slant. Their thoughts weren't hinged together, so naturally they'd have slightly different viewpoints. She wasn't annoyed with him for introducing a note of fun to a dilemma that scraped Eve's tender heart to the raw and offered no solution at all. She could weep into her fingers and the end result would be the same as Paul's slightly callous laughter. Except that he didn't mean to be callous. It would take a man of rare sensitivity to see the situation through a woman's emotions. No, what fretted her most grievously was that Paul, for all his damnable masculine insensitivity, was infuriatingly right.

It incensed her to admit it, but it was better to go along with the delusion that Alice Meakin was dotty, if that was the only way of keeping Bert intact upon his pedestal. It was important to keep the memory pure and unsullied. It was the first time in her life that she had owned, even to herself, that a lie, even one by deviation, was superior to the truth.

Suddenly, she felt her chin being taken and lifted. And she knew, as if the knowledge came to her through the fingertips turning her face, how it would be with Paul. Not for him Hubert Rowland's noble self-denial. Paul wouldn't be content to know his love was all right, he'd want to feel she was right in his arms.

Coming into the warm flush of her thoughts, Paul's voice sounded very dry. 'I think we'd better go and get that drink and cocktail savoury, before it turns into a slice of toast and a glass of orange juice. If we delay much longer we'll just be in time for breakfast.'

7

'We'd just about given you up,' said Lilith Brookes, opening the door to them.

Eve sensed that behind the polite blankness of Lilith's eyes was a lively speculation. Had she been taken aback when Paul asked for her name to be included in the invitation? Was she surprised that their friendship extended beyond the schoolroom? Surprised and — Eve's sharp eye saw a slight pruning of the mouth — displeased? But what could it matter to Lilith Brookes what she was — or hoped to be — to Paul?

The expression that Eve may only have imagined, melted with the receding darkness as Lilith's welcome exploded into sparkling hostess proportions, pulling them from the shadowy recess of the door into the brightly lit hall.

'Enter, you charming people.'

Eve was struck by the friendly spontaneity, which couldn't have been in more direct contrast to their last meeting, when Eve couldn't spare the time to stop and talk because she was in a hurry to get to the station to meet Shelley Anne's train.

'Miss Masters, you look delightful. Doesn't she Paul?'

The hand holding Eve's gave it a little squeeze.

'I think so.'

Eve wondered what they were letting themselves in for. The noise that had assaulted their ears on getting out of the car, was now quite deafening.

'I'm sorry we're late,' Paul apologised.

'As if that matters now that you're here,' replied their hostess. 'The party has hardly begun.'

Party! Eve had anticipated a few people in for drinks. And had considered that the ultimate in torture.

Paul's mouth fixed in a smile. 'Come on,' he coaxed Eve, 'let's join in the fun.'

Almost immediately Lilith annexed Paul, and Nicholas Brookes took charge of her. 'Good evening, Miss Masters. How nice of Paul to bring you,' he said.

'It was kind of you to invite me.'

The room was so crowded that within seconds Paul and Lilith disappeared from her sight.

'May I call you Eve? One cannot be formal at a party.'

'Please do.'

'Then you must call me Nick. That's a fair exchange, isn't it?'

It might be, but Eve preferred to know people better before using their first names. Short as his name was, it would be a formidable mouthful. She swallowed and said: 'All right.' And if Nicholas Brookes noticed she didn't say, 'All right, Nick,' he did not comment upon it.

'My daughter thinks very highly of you, Eve.'

'Oh?'

'What's that supposed to mean?'

'Nothing.' But it hadn't been just an answering murmur; more of a disbelieving grunt. As if she thought he'd never been concerned enough to find out what his daughter thought deep down.

Nicholas Brookes was nobody's fool. His eyebrows manoeuvred into shrewd peaks. 'Would a change of subject be to my advantage? I've an unpleasant feeling that to continue with the present one would be the same thing as inviting you to . . .'

'To what?' said Paul, who had skipped Lilith's net to stroll back and join them.

'Not that sort of invitation old man, so no need to get jealous.'

If only Paul were jealous! To be jealous one must know a warmer, worthier emotion.

Something bubbling and irrepressible — she would never know what! — made Eve drawl provocatively: 'How very dashing for my hopes. I'm devastated!'

Both men laughed, Nick's laughter

being the loudest even though his eyes acknowledged that she'd scored off him. All unease was brushed away, but how much better she would have liked it had Paul's laughter been edged with strain.

'What I was going to say before I was so entertainingly interrupted, was that to continue with the conversation as it was, would be to invite Eve to trot out my many shortcomings as a parent. You can believe it or not, but we were talking about my daughter.'

'As you say,' said Paul. 'The choice is mine. To believe or not.'

Out of the blue, Nick said: 'I'm sorry, Paul. When I asked you to drop in I really did think it was one or two people for drinks. It was Lilith's idea to turn it into a party. You know Lilith.'

'Yes,' acknowledged Paul in such a dry tone that Eve was clued to the fact that it wasn't just an idle remark. Paul *knew* Lilith, knew her not just as the wife of a good friend but . . . From the beginning, almost, she'd known there was a girl in Paul's past, someone he'd cared very much about and who had hurt him deeply. Could that girl be Lilith? Had Lilith actually chosen between Paul and Nick? But . . . she moved her chin in a small shake of bewilderment. It didn't make sense. How could anyone with even half an eye and the smallest grain of sense prefer Nick to Paul?

She didn't realise that Nick had gone until a strong brown finger forced up her chin. Peaty brown eyes smouldered into hers. 'Don't ever try anything like that on with the likes of Nick again, my girl.'

If only she was. His girl. Hope expanded her heart to twice its size.

'What do you mean? Nick's your friend. Anyway, he's married.'

'Do you think being married makes a hoot of difference to some people?'

To some people it wouldn't matter. But it mattered to Paul. Whatever he'd been to Lilith had been buried when she chose Nicholas Brookes.

Once again she'd become separated from Paul. As before, Lilith had claimed him; this time Eve's view of the pair of them was not so obscured that she couldn't see the dark head bent in an attentively listening angle above a sweetly tilted profile. The amity they now enjoyed spelt it out to her that Paul had come to terms with her marriage to Nicholas Brookes. One dismaying aspect stayed in Eve's head. She did not see how Paul could ever come to love her . . . not if Lilith was the type of woman he found himself attracted to.

Someone was watching her. So strongly did she get that eyes boring into the back of her neck sensation that she stiffened to her fingertips. She started to turn her neck, slowly. Stopping when her vision rested on a pair of grey-green eyes in a laughing, handsome face. Recognising the suave, Bohemian dressed Samaritan who had come to her's and Shelley Anne's aid at the railway station, Eve's mouth broke into a reciprocating smile.

And now Tony Adamson was striding towards her. 'I've been willing you to look at me for the last five minutes.'

Five minutes used figuratively? Or had he really been observing her for that length of time? If so he must have seen the way she'd been looking at Paul and Lilith.

'They make a handsome pair, don't they?' said Tony, telling her the worst.

'How did you come to be invited?' said Eve, putting on a bright face. 'Are you a friend of Lilith's or Nick's?'

'Are you in love with him?' said Tony, pursuing his own line of questioning.

'With Nick?' — Attempting to inject a note of ridicule.

'With the schoolmaster? You don't need to answer. Your face has already answered for you. Are you free to accept an invitation to come out to dinner with me one evening?'

Which, Eve thought, was rather a subtle way of asking if she had an understanding with Paul. He even

160

darted a look at her left hand.

'As free as air, but . . . '

'Go on.'

'I won't be very good company.'

'Let me be the best judge of that. If, by not being good company, it means you won't be fluttering your lashes at me and drooling over everything I say, that's splendid. Will it sound terribly conceited if I say that it will make a refreshing change?'

'Terribly conceited. Do women flutter their eyelashes at you and drool?'

'All the time. It's a dreadful bore.' And then, going on to answer the lift of her eyebrows. 'Man enjoys the hunt. What enjoyment is there in chasing a willing prey?'

'I never looked at it that way. I thought men exulted in feminine adoration.'

'It is flattering, I won't deny. But it can also be frightening. Your sex is so aggressive these days.'

'Oh, poor you. If you go on like this, you'll have me sobbing into my sherry.'

'Is that what you're drinking. Shall I get you another one?'

'No thanks. I'm perfectly content.'

'Yes, you are that unusual combination. A contented female. Apart from wanting the schoolmaster, that is. Incidentally, he's bearing down on us, and so our delicious conversation must come to an end. Quickly, are you doing anything tomorrow?'

'Why . . . er . . . no.'

'Good. I'll call for you at seven-thirty. Is it on?'

It wasn't really on for her to make a date with Tony.

'Yes,' she said with sparkling decision. It was fun to plan a meeting with one man under the nose of another.

'Hello, Paul,' she said, wondering if he'd heard Tony making a date with her. A spark of the Jezebel that lurks in every woman, hoped he had. Or was she getting her own back because of his suspected interest in Lilith? 'Have you met the artist in our midst? Tony Adamson — Paul Smalley.'

162

The handshake was accompanied by lively amusement on Tony's part, and wary summing-up on Paul's.

'Local gossip has it you're from London,' said Paul, frowning and so displaying not a scrap of the charm that could have lifted his square, craggy features up to, say, Tony's level of good looks.

Oh dear, Eve thought with that sinking feeling inside. Woman-like she'd wanted to show Paul off a little. Instead she felt shown up by an obdurance that was sliding into hostility.

'London was my last abode,' said Tony, his smiling manner a sharp, delightful contrast. 'But I don't hail from there.'

'Your face seems familiar. Have we met before?' The question was shot with bullet direction, its driving force considerably more than polite enquiry. Whatever was going on behind Paul's scowling brow was digging deep.

'We haven't met, otherwise I would have remembered,' said Tony.

'Humph! Not too sure about that. There's something about your face that's — ' At last his glance clashed with Eve's. To her tremendous relief, because Paul's eagle penetration was beginning to be embarrassing, he said: 'It doesn't matter. How long are you planning to be with us?'

'Depends.'

'On?' probed Paul, causing Eve to wriggle again.

'Things. Been nice talking to you . . . but I see I'm being signalled across the room.

Although Eve turned her head immediately, she could not see any beckoning fingers. The constraint Tony's presence had induced, remained even now his vibrant personality was removed.

'Wonder what he's up to?' Paul observed meditatively.

'Does he have to be up to anything?'

'Come on, Eve. Even you must have noticed how cagey he was. He didn't want to answer any pertinent questions.'

164

'Don't you think you're being a tiny bit absurd?' said Eve in the sort of crackle-brittle tone that yesterday she couldn't have imagined using on Paul. 'You've taken an intense, and to my mind completely unfounded dislike of the man. Don't try to square yourself by daubing him as an impostor.'

'Is that what you think?' said Paul, the space between his eyebrows narrowing. 'Seems to me you've taken quite a shine to the fellow.'

'I think he's a nice, pleasant young man, and I can't understand your attitude.'

'Nor I yours. I can't understand why you've agreed to go out with him tomorrow.'

'So you did hear,' she hissed in bitter joy. 'Surely that isn't what this is all about?'

'Now you're the one who's being absurd. What you do out of school hours is none of my business.'

'No it isn't,' she flashed spiritedly. 'High time you remembered.'

'What a party this is turning out to be! I'm leaving. Are you coming with me, or will Tony be escorting you home? Perhaps you'd prefer that!'

'Perhaps I would!' Eve was stung to retort. 'Perhaps I would at that.' Her voice was wild and high and she wouldn't let him see that the blaze of anger in her eyes was brightened by tears.

She had no idea how this combustible situation had developed, or how to stop it flaring into a raging holocaust that would destroy everything that was sweet and worthwhile between them. And her stomach muscles were gripped by such excitement, an elation she had never known before. Paul was jealous. Absurdly, needlessly, wonderfully jealous.

'Fetch your coat,' he ordered. The command touched her heart as it penetrated her ears. His eyes were saying, 'I can't wait to get you outside.' There was not the slightest possibility of her mistaking just what he had in mind once he got her there.

She nodded mindlessly, and submitted her legs to the task of wobbling weakly through the throng, up the stairs to the bedroom where the female guests' coats had been spirited away to. Her mouth was burning and all her nerve ends were on fire, and she didn't know how she was going to curtail her longing until she was back by his side. In her mind's eye she saw the sweet, dark passion smouldering in his eyes.

Her steps broke into a run. She tumbled the coats in her haste to find hers, eventually slinging it round her shoulders and starting back down when she heard her name being called, so softly. As soft as imagination.

She thought it was imagination, and started to walk again, when an urgent: 'Miss . . . Miss Masters . . . please Miss,' halted her step.

Turning, she saw a white triangle of face in the wedge of darkness cast by a partially opened door.

'Hello Charlotte.'

'Will you come in and talk to me for a minute?'

'I . . . can't.' But even as she said that she was weakening, because the pleading in the young voice was a blow to the heart. A different sort of blow to the one Paul had just rendered it, but effective enough in its own right.

'I've got a present I want to give you.'

'Oh Charlotte.' Her voice was dismayed. Didn't she know that people couldn't be bought? She took a step forward.

As Charlotte thrust the door open wider for Eve to enter, the light from the long landing-passage fell like a golden sword across the luxury bedroom of any girl's dreams. Envy was not totally absent from Eve's eye as she picked out a white, ceiling-high bedroom fitment with a gilt trim, a carpet of deep cornflower blue and curtains and bedspread to match. The bedside rug was white lambswool and the bookcase was filled with enough books to delight even Eve's thirst for reading.

Oh you lucky, lucky girl. Why can't you be satisfied with all this? Why do you want what even the most deprived child in my class takes as his/her right? The tender, bruising, taking, giving, down to earth very real love of a mother. Even poor little to-be-pitied Cheryl Carter was not as deprived as this. In her own rough way, Betty Carter saw to it that Cheryl knew she was loved.

The voices in her head began to weep silently. Eve, very much aware that Paul was waiting downstairs, knew he must cool his impatience, as she must cool hers. She must spare Charlotte these few minutes.

'Look Miss. This is my present to you.'

'I don't want a present, Charlotte. It isn't necessary. You don't have to give people anything. All that it takes to be liked is to be your own sweet, natural self.' Eve didn't know whether to hug Charlotte or shake her. Short of taking up a hammer, how could she get through to the girl that once she stopped trying so intensely, stopped forcing herself on people, she would begin to be accepted?

Charlotte darted across to switch on the bedside lamp. Eve gently closed the door and followed, her movements slow, giving herself time to think.

'It's only a small present, Miss.' The eagerness in the out thrust hand was matched by the earnestness of the appeal in Charlotte's rounded eyes.

'No, Charlotte. Can't you take in what I'm trying to tell you?'

'Please . . . look.'

'Yes, of course I'll . . . Charlotte dear, you're crying. What is it?' She brushed the hair away from Charlotte's flushed, tense face, willing herself to be accurate in her reading of the expression in the tear-brilliant eyes. Their blueness like sapphires that melted into Eve's brain.

Her hands dropped to the slender

shoulders, her eyes to the object in Charlotte's hand. What she saw there dried the breath in her throat; a million and one explanations buzzed in her head.

'Charlotte, you must tell me the truth. Where did you get this from?'

'I bought it for you, of course.'

'A brooch like this costs a great deal of money.'

A mumble.

'What did you say, dear?'

'I said not all that much.'

But it had. Eve knew exactly how much it had cost, because she had priced it that morning in her friend Avril's curio shop, and it was considerably beyond her means. Beyond Charlotte's too.

The object that lay in Charlotte's hand, the present she was intent on giving Eve, was the rose brooch. The brooch Eve had so much ached to possess that its delicate beauty, each exquisitely furled petal, was indelibly printed on her mind. Last seen on a pad of black velvet in Avril's carelessly unlocked showcase. Oh, Avril, you should have been more vigilant. You knew the showcase was unlocked. We talked about it. It must have been at the back of my mind that . . .

No, I must not condemn Charlotte until I am absolutely sure. This isn't Avril's brooch, but a clever, cheap imitation. But it was a forlorn hope.

Why did it have to be the rose brooch? Why that? Any other blessed thing and Eve would not have looked beyond the gift. Wouldn't have had to probe in this hateful, distressing way.

'Where did you buy it, Charlotte?'

'From Avril's.'

'When?'

'This hometime, after school.'

'Was . . . ' careful swallow . . . 'anyone with you?'

'Cheryl Carter. But she didn't see, I bought it while her back was turned.'

'I don't think that is quite the truth, is it, Charlotte?'

No reply. Not even a mumble. But

the eyes were heavy with guilt. No less heavy than the weight of this terrible thing Eve had uncovered and so had become her burden. She would not shirk it.

'Oh Charlotte, my poor deluded, sweet little girl. You know you can tell me.'

'I'm not s-sweet. I'm h-horrid.'

'No you're not.'

'Y-you d-don't know.'

'I do know, Charlotte.'

As she held Charlotte close, she thought how small and thin the stiff, resisting body felt. As Charlotte tried to draw away, she tightened her hold. Suddenly the childish form went slack, and the tears poured out of her with a vengeance, petering out after a time into harsh, shuddering sobs.

'I took — '

'I know, dear. Don't worry, we'll sort it all out. Relax, sweetheart, it will be all right.'

'It w-was s-so easy.'

'I know. I know.'

The head came up from Eve's shoulder. 'Will you tell Daddy and *her*?'

The stressed 'her' was dismayingly significant.

'In the morning. I'm not going to bother them in the middle of their party. The brooch must be returned to Avril. For the time being, I'll take charge of it, shall I?' Eve slid the brooch into her handbag, closing it with a decisive snap. 'There now. Let's have you back into bed. Things won't seem half as bad after a good night's sleep.'

'Will I . . . ' An anguished eye blinked open . . . 'go to prison?'

'Good heaven's no. Off with your dressing gown. That's a good girl. Now, hop into bed.' Odd how you can talk to a fifteen year old as though she were six in times of trouble.

Charlotte hopped.

'Will you stay with me for a while?'

'All right, if it will make you feel better.'

Apparently it did, because Charlotte managed a watery smile and snuggled down under the bed covers. Eve sat in a chair that was deep and comfortable. Looking at the drowsy little face she thought it wouldn't be long before Charlotte was asleep. She heard the noise of the party going on below, where Paul would be waiting for her and wondering where she had got to. Her brain was whirling. The 'if onlys' and 'why didn'ts' tumbled and eddied like the seeds of a blown dandelion clock, until her thoughts became a confusion of recriminations and regrets. Thought after thought lost itself in a blizzard of disjointed beginnings that couldn't germinate and take root. As if her mind found the effort of it all just too much.

The distasteful scene had taken a bigger toll than she realised. Her eyelids were growing heavier and heavier and her head felt too weighty for her neck to support. Gratefully she let the back of the chair take the strain. Her eyelids succumbed. She was asleep.

She had no way of knowing how long she slept. When she woke the bedside lamp no longer spread its soft glow, her neck had a crick in it, and one foot was numb. She was vaguely aware that she had been dreaming about Paul. She slid her foot out of her shoe and rubbed it to restore the circulation, and only then did she realise that someone else had come into the room and was studying her intently.

'Well, well!' said Lilith Brookes, her forehead wrinkling delicately back in amusement.

'I'm so sorry. I . . . I fell asleep.'

'Don't apologise. I'm delighted to be such a successful hostess, making my guests feel so at home.'

It seeped through to Eve, slowly, that Lilith was in her nightgown.

'Oh dear! Everyone must have left ages ago. Paul?'

'Thought you'd exercised woman's prerogative.'

'I don't understand what you mean.'

Eve was falling-about awkward. Not only did the situation she found herself in put her at a disadvantage, she was not properly awake.

'Of changing her mind. Coincidentally, as it turned out, Tony Adamson disappeared at the same time, and Paul naturally thought . . .'

'I'd gone home with Tony.'

'You must admit it did seem the obvious conclusion. Especially as . . .'

Eve's chin tilted in askance.

'Well, you'd been playing one off against the other. For one skilled in such artistry that can be a worthwhile and amusing game. The timid and the innocent are better not participating because not only must it be played with great panache, but it must be carried out with daring and sophistication in order to avoid the pitfalls, the dangers. And you are not at all proficient in such matters, are you? In fact you are as innocent as your namesake, before . . . But I don't have to go into that because I'm sure you know your bible.

Ah yes! All very touching. It hurts me to have to tell you how angry Paul is with you.'

'*Is* he?'

'You aren't meant to sound flattered. A man's feelings do not have to be emotionally aroused for him to be annoyed when a woman shows a preference for another man. Men are born rivals. When a woman openly shuns one in favour of another, he feels that his masculine pride has been attacked, and that is the most cruel thing a foolish woman can do. A foolish woman, because a clever woman always safeguards against the ultimate destruction.'

'And you are a very clever woman indeed,' said Eve, climbing off her whipping block, and swinging her chin high in dignity. 'Don't you ever make a mistake?'

It had been a mistake, a horrible, ghastly mistake to try to make Paul jealous. Her stratagem — or lack of it — had failed miserably. And miserable was how Eve felt.

But it wasn't solely *her* doing that had put that beautiful warmth, that volcanic, smouldering passion in jeopardy. A child had cried out, and she had answered that cry. Given the hours back she wouldn't have it any other way. But, oh, to have acted so selflessly and to feel so cruelly punished!

This last piece of folly was just something else to be explained in the morning she hadn't the strength to face.

8

Lilith Brookes looked at Eve with open enmity in her eyes. There was no flippant answer to Eve's, 'Don't you ever make a mistake?'

It hadn't even been a clever shaft. Lilith could have admired her for that. Knowing that Eve had struck out blindly in retaliation made it harder to swallow.

'Yes, I made a mistake,' Lilith said coldly. 'I married the wrong man. Did you know that Paul and I were once very close?'

'Do you mean you should have married Paul?'

Lilith's iced smile neither assented, nor denied. 'I'll put some clothes on and run you home,' she said.

'Thank you.' Eve looked miserable. 'I'm sorry to be such a nuisance. It's very kind of you.'

Kind? Kind? Didn't the silly girl know she couldn't wait to get her out of the house?

'I'll throw on a pair of slacks and a sweater. Wait downstairs for me.'

Something in Eve rebelled. 'There's no need for you to drive me home. I . . . I could sleep on the sofa in the lounge, and catch a bus as soon as it's daylight.'

Lilith drew herself up to her full height. 'Don't be ridiculous,' she said, as though with extreme satisfaction. 'It's not going to do your reputation as a schoolmistress much good if you're seen tom-catting it home at first light.'

As the logic of that was undoubtedly sound, Eve gave in. With far more grace than Lilith employed in executing the favour.

In the unaccustomed luxury of Lilith's E-Type Jaguar, Eve gave a fleeting thought to the recovered loot in her handbag. Had Lilith been a more sympathetic stepmother, she might have told her about the brooch. She might have told her anyway if there hadn't been something in Lilith's manner that scratched her nerves to the raw. A bitter hostility that wasn't conducive to confidences of any nature, let alone one of unpleasant content.

The church clock was striking four as the Jaguar whispered to a halt outside Eve's front door. Eve didn't see a curtain twitching in a window across the street. 'Thank you and goodnight,' she said, alighting.

'That's all right,' said Lilith, grudgingly. Driving away before Eve had inserted her key in the lock.

Eve didn't think she would sleep. To her horror she overslept. This day of all days. She looked at the clock, rubbing her eyes, and groaning in disbelief. She had intended getting up especially early to call in on Avril and return the brooch, with luck before the loss was discovered, and still have time to make her peace with Paul before morning assembly.

Faced with the two alternatives, Eve

decided it would be better to see Avril and get the wretched brooch back to her, even if it meant being late for school. But — and she couldn't remember this ever happening before — the shop was still locked up. Eve rattled the door, but there was no sign of Avril. No consolation, either, that she wasn't the only one to sleep in, because it meant taking the brooch to school with her.

The children had already filed into the big hall by the time she arrived. Eve scanned the faces of both teachers and pupils alike. No Paul yet, and no Charlotte Brookes either. Not that Eve had expected Charlotte to turn up for school this morning. Had Charlotte told her father and stepmother the truth, Eve wondered, or had she invented some indisposition?

The moment assembly was over, Eve must see Paul. She must go to him and tell him everything and ask to be excused in her free period so that she could slip up the road to Avril's to return the brooch. Lunchtime might be too late.

Miss Meakin was standing primly on one side of the platform. Very tall and slim and straight-backed. Rigidly upright in both her bearing and the way she conducted her life. Difficult to rub out the years and imagine her soft and dewy for her wartime sweetheart. Clinging to him, perhaps, in a tearful goodbye. Believing his promise to marry her, mooning over his ring. All these years sustained on a false memory. The sheer, *pitiful* waste of it all!

For a little while, after meeting Hubert Rowland and liking him, and talking about him afterwards to Paul, Eve had drifted into her own make-believe and had thought that despite the obstacle of his marriage they could still find their happiness together. But now that the romantic spell of evening was removed, Eve knew that Paul was right and that it could never be.

Hopefully, she cast a smile in Alice

Meakin's direction. Alice Meakin's head turned away, although she was perfectly aware that Eve was trying to catch her eye.

It was the old story of a confidence given in the heat of the moment, and later regretted. The weakness of confiding in a young and foolish girl had kept Alice Meakin's eyes open for most of the night. She had sat by her bedroom window, annoyed with herself, and even more annoyed with Eve for being so receptive and sympathetic, coaxing the indiscretion out of her. When all the time the flighty little madam couldn't wait to be rid of her and her romantic bletherings so that she could dolly herself up for a night on the tiles.

The girl's innocent look had fooled her for a time, but now she had her measure. Rolling home at four o'clock in the morning in a big, expensive car. A time when all decent people should be in their beds, never mind a girl who was entrusted to shape the moral character of Hawsbury's impressionable youth.

In keeping with her generation, Alice Meakin wasn't overly car conscious, not like young people of today who can identify any car, even the foreign makes, instantly. She couldn't tell one car from another, and even prided herself on her indifference. But it had registered in her mind that the car which had conveyed Eve home was long and expensive looking and darkish in colour. She had concentrated her efforts on seeing who was behind the steering wheel, but her hoped-for glimpse of him had been thwarted because he hadn't been chivalrous enough to get out of the car and see Eve to her door.

Fancy telling a girl who came home at that hour about her Bert. As if she would understand the bitter-sweet, Spring-like innocence of their love. Bert . . . who had cherished her to her fingertips and had respected, as any gentleman should, the strictures of her God-fearing upbringing. 'One day, Bert, it will be as you want. We will be everything to each other,' her eyes had promised. And all these years she'd kept herself for him, waiting, hoping . . .

★ ★ ★

Assembly was nearly over. Eve could now dare to creep out before the charging herd and nail Paul, assuming he was in his study, and get this dreadful thing off her chest.

Paul was in his study, but he was not alone. An argument was ripping away behind the closed door. Even as she hesitated, the door cracked open and two men came out, with Paul hot on their heels.

'Yes, I appreciate you are doing your duty, but just see you keep me informed,' Paul said darkly, his tone veering strongly towards threat.

'We'll do our best,' placated the older of the two men.

There was something so official about

187

it all that Eve should have known she was already too late. But she did not associate the men, who were in ordinary clothes, with police officers.

'Yes?' Paul said to Eve, on a note of cool enquiry. 'What can I do for you, taking into account that you are due in class in two minutes' time?'

Stung by his impersonal attitude and censorious tone, she said: 'I know all about that, Paul, but this is important.' And then, foolishly putting aside her unpleasant mission, she enquired: 'You're not angry with me, are you, about last night? Because I can explain.'

'Angry? What an absurd notion! Why should I be angry because the girl I took to a party preferred to go home with someone else?'

'I didn't go off with Tony.'

His brow arched. 'Tony's simultaneous exit being a coincidence?'

'If you like. You can put what explanation to that you damn well please, but it will be wrong if you think it had anything to do with me,' she said, recoiling from the glitter of ice in his eye and the lilt of sarcasm in his tone. This was a Paul she had never seen before, hard and without tenderness. Squaring her shoulders she said: 'I expected better of you than this.'

'Shouldn't that be my line?' he parried.

'Please don't be so cynical and allow me to explain what happened.'

'Sorry, but no. Explanations are tedious. I'd rather leave things as they are. In a way, I feel grateful to Tony.' A nerve jumped at the side of his mouth and her fingers reacted by aching to reach up and smooth the hurt and tension away. 'I was in danger of making a bigger fool of myself if Tony hadn't enticed you away. I thought that you and I . . . that we . . . but it doesn't matter now.'

An instinctive feeling of sympathy for anyone who fell foul of jealousy's ire was being swamped by incredulous wonder. 'Oh, Paul, it *does* matter.'

His hands came out to trap her wrists, and move slowly up to her elbows. For a glorious, blood-pounding moment she thought he was going to continue easing her forward until he'd drawn her all the way into his arms. Instead, he held her an abrupt elbow length away and probed her eyes in a long searching glance that was a death potion to her newly awakened hopes. Better that he'd seared her lips with brutal, punishing kisses than shower her with lukewarm understanding. Forgiveness was no salvation when it was levied in such detached tones.

'Girls of your age should be free to flirt around. The mistake was mine for forgetting that.'

'You're making a bigger mistake if you believe that,' she blazed at him through clenched teeth.

'I'm trying to tell you I don't blame you for what happened.'

'How can you blame me or not blame me when you won't listen to what happened.' Her hazel eyes were burning and intense; her mind was such an unhappy fuzz of frustration she found it difficult to think coherently. Instead of waffling on like an imbecile, there was something important she should be telling Paul.

Still holding her arm, quite gently he piloted her to the door.

Eve marked the register, noting that Cheryl Carter was absent again. It was too distressing of her mother to keep her away like this. She set the first lesson. She wasn't concentrating very well. If only she hadn't fallen asleep last night in Charlotte's bedroom. Something was bothering her about that, but she didn't know what. Something . . .

If Lilith had discovered her sooner; say she'd looked in on Charlotte to say goodnight and turn out the light, the sort of thing even a not very diligent stepmother would do, it wouldn't have been so late that she couldn't phone Paul. 'Look, I've done something stupid. I looked in on

Charlotte and I fell asleep. Will you come back for me?'

The thing that was very wrong might have occurred to Eve then as the events of the previous evening flashed in a series of picture stills behind her eyes, if she hadn't remembered something more dismaying. The brooch was still in her handbag. She hadn't told Paul about it, and the longer she delayed, the greater the risk of Avril discovering the loss. In the muddle of her thoughts was the fact that she didn't want to cause Avril any unnecessary distress.

Instructing the class to continue on their own, she scooped up her handbag and marched briskly along the corridor to Paul's study. Only to find it vacant. What to do?

Get the brooch back to Avril, and face the other consequences later. She collected her coat from the staff room, whisked back down the corridor and out of the school doors, feeling as guilty as a reluctant pupil skiving a lesson. She knew that even if Avril agreed to take no action, she would still have to report the matter to Paul for Charlotte's own good. Charlotte's taking the brooch had been a cry for help. Bless her, she was so unhappy she'd do anything to be noticed.

Because she was an intelligent girl, she would have worked it out that the theft was bound to be discovered. Hadn't she tempted discovery in offering the brooch to Eve, Avril's best friend?

To Eve's astonishment, Avril was outside her shop, on the point of locking it up. Unheard of at mid morning.

'Where are you dashing off to?'

'Eve, are you coming with me?' said Avril, barely hearing. 'How darling of you. Of course, you would be concerned, the girl being a pupil of yours. Oh, Eve, I feel so dreadful about this. You will believe I acted without thinking? I couldn't bear it if you thought badly of me. I did it on impulse. At the time I was too flaming mad to think straight, and I acted automatically.'

'Just what course did this automatic action take?'

'Cut the smart talk, Eve, I can't stand it.'

'I'm not being smart. I honestly don't know what you're talking about.'

'But you must know. You're here because of the theft of the brooch, aren't you?'

'You know about *that*?' Eve said faintly.

'Don't be dim. Didn't I see that it was missing the moment those two tykes left my shop? I knew the law wouldn't be able to do much in the way of punishment, because when it came to it I'd no intention of pressing charges. But I thought a visit from the police might put the fear of God into the silly little madam and prevent her ending up in real trouble. I didn't think her dad was going to come the heavy Victorian father. Don't think he meant to either. Apparently, he raised his hand as if to go for her and she sort of fell back, trying to get out of the way I suppose, which is a natural reaction and — ' pausing for breath — 'are you all right, Eve? You've gone just like death. You *did* know about it, didn't you?'

'Yes. No. Not that you'd found out. Just that the brooch had been taken. She was . . . you wouldn't believe this . . . but she wanted to give it to me as a present.'

'She didn't! She must have known . . . '

' . . . that it would all come out? Yes, I reasoned that out, too. So, for attention, do you think? Good grief, the poor kid's been crying out to be noticed long enough. Anyway, to cut a long story short, we had a little talk and I said I'd slip the brooch back to you and no harm done. So — here,' — delving into her handbag. 'Take it. I just feel bitter and angry with myself that I wasn't soon enough to prevent this rumpus.'

'Don't distress yourself, Eve. Because I've a feeling it still wouldn't have been soon enough. When did your heart-to-heart take place?'

'Oh, some time about midnight.'

'There, then! If it'll make you feel any better, I discovered the theft not long after school let out, and that's when I got the police in.'

'I'm a bit muddled. When did the police visit the girl's house?'

'Straight away. It isn't good to let any grass grow under the feet in such matters. I do believe that you and I might have got our wires crossed. When did you talk to Cheryl? When the police talked to her she denied taking the brooch . . . yet she gave it to you. I don't understand,' admitted Avril, thoroughly mystified.

'What's Cheryl Carter got to do with it?' said Eve, no less puzzled.

'Didn't . . .' biting her lip and fearfully hesitant . . . 'Cheryl take the brooch?'

'No. Charlotte Brookes did.'

'No. You're making a mistake, Eve. You are, aren't you? It just isn't possible. Oh no!' Avril had looked green about the matter all along; now, not only did she look sickly, but wildly distraught. Her mouth was a ring of pain and when she started to speak again there was a quaver in her voice. 'This is worse than I thought. The two kids were in the shop at the same time, and nobody would think to accuse Charlotte Brookes of . . . '

'Theft,' supplied Eve, when it became obvious her friend found the word too torturous to get out.

'Don't look at me like that, Eve. Put yourself in my place, knowing that Nicholas Brookes would have bought her the wretched brooch, or any other blessed thing shc'd set her heart on. She doesn't have to . . . '

'Steal,' said Eve, ruthlessly.

'Charlotte isn't the type of girl to . . . ' It seemed that Avril was incapable of completing a sentence.

'And poor Cheryl Carter is?' pressed Eve. 'She's branded as a likely suspect because she hasn't got a rich father to indulge her every whim and smother her with expensive gifts. Look Avril — ' taking pity on her friend, who had acted stupidly but not with malicious intent — 'if it's any consolation, I'm not whipping you any more than I'm whipping myself. I've seen this situation building up, and I haven't done a thing about it. I've known that Charlotte was finding it difficult to come to terms with having a stepmother and that she desperately needed help. But I needed this sort of spur before I'd think of interfering. It's all too dreadful.'

'It's even more dreadful than you think,' said Avril in a terrifyingly quiet voice. 'I thought you knew. I thought Paul must have told you and sent you along, because they phoned him first to tell him . . . '

'Tell him what?' Eve's brain was spinning into action. She'd heard the telephone ringing as she'd walked away from Paul's study the first time. This would be the phone call Avril referred to. What was the content of this phone call that had caused Paul to rush off somewhere, and was subjecting Avril to such distress?

Tongues of fear licked her throat dry as precognition flew beyond this dreadful thing Avril was about to tell her, and her mind was struck rigid with shock. But even in this grey grip of inertia there was an inner hammering on memory's closed door. Something . . . some mysterious knowledge running sickly through her. A force that would keep her in its petrified grip until something within the scope of her own memory broke its dark spell.

Avril's haunted eyes, resembling two charred holes in a white mask, filmed over with tears. 'When Cheryl's father went as if to strike her, in twisting out of reach she over-balanced and fell, hitting her head. She was a bit whooshy last night, but it was thought all right to put her to bed, although Jack and Betty Carter fully intended taking her to hospital for a check this morning.

But when Betty went into her bedroom, there was no sign of Cheryl. It wasn't until they'd contacted the police, and the police asked for a check on her wardrobe to establish what Cheryl was wearing, that it was realised none of her clothes was missing. It would seem that a mildly concussed girl is roaming about in her nightie.'

★ ★ ★

Avril and Eve ran into Paul as he was coming out of the police station. He shook his head on seeing their worried faces. 'There's a full alert out, but no news yet. The fear is that Cheryl could have been missing since last night. It's possible she could be lying somewhere in a coma. Cracks on the head such as she inflicted on herself are funny things, but no point in going over that again. Betty and Jack Carter are punishing themselves enough on that account.'

'Cheryl didn't even take the brooch,'

said Avril, choking to have to tell him.

'She didn't?' Paul's face was a black mask of enquiry as he looked from one girl to the other.

'It was Charlotte Brookes who took it,' Eve elected to explain. 'When I went up for my coat last night, Charlotte called me into her bedroom and tried to make me a gift of the stolen brooch. I recognised it as being one I'd been tempted to buy that same day, and taxed her about how it came to be in her possession. She admitted taking it from Avril's showcase.'

'We could be looking for Cheryl. Couldn't we talk later?'

'No . . . there's a tie somewhere.' Eve commanded herself to think. And, as in a miracle, all the grey shapes in Eve's mind lumped together and exploded into one bright thought. 'Cheryl would know she hadn't taken the brooch, so she'd start to wonder who had. And, perhaps, even in her dazed condition, she'd remember that Charlotte was in the shop with her.'

'So, despite her distressed state of mind, even though she was too bemused to think about putting on clothes, she set off to walk to Charlotte's,' said Paul, warming to the theory.

'And might be lying somewhere, probably unconscious, on the moorland road she would have to take to get to Charlotte's house,' reasoned Eve.

But it was not logic that made either her or Paul want to search one particular spot in all the vast moor. Both of them remembered, almost at the same time, Eve's strange behaviour as they had crossed a certain stretch of the moor yesterday evening, almost as if she had had a presentiment of the tragedy about to take place.

'It will be uncanny, to say the least,' said Paul, bundling both girls into his car. 'And nobody would believe how we knew, if we lost all leave of our senses and were ill-advised enough to tell, that is.'

'If she's there,' Eve cautioned, knowing

with a skin-crawling certainty they would find Cheryl not far from the spot where she had had such a strange sensation yesterday evening.

'What on earth are the pair of you talking about?' Although Avril's query was reasonable, Paul brushed it to oneside. Never for a second slackening speed, he started to question Eve.

'Let me get this straight. You say you took possession of the brooch last night?'

'Yes.'

'Why didn't you tell me this when you came to my study this morning?'

'I tried to, but — '

'You got side-tracked by a more important issue, is that it?'

'You know that's not it at all and it's horrid of you to suggest it. You wouldn't let me speak. You hustled me out.'

'Looking at this objectively, it still seems you gave your own petty doings greater priority.'

'If you mean by 'my petty doings'

the assumption that's stuck mulishly in your head that Tony Adamson took me home last night, my answer is still the same. He didn't. As the one thing seemed to be tied up with the other, I was trying to get that out of the way first. But you wouldn't listen.'

'I'm listening now.'

Her heart dropped like a stone and spread ripples of agony through her body. Explanations of a confessional nature require to be levied in an atmosphere of warmth and understanding. There was nothing in Paul's face to give her even a finger-hold of comfort. And no solace in the fact that she was pleading to be believed by someone who was making it blatantly obvious he had no trust in her.

Wretchedly she repeated the sorry tale of going for her coat and being waylaid by Charlotte, and the regrettable business of the brooch.

Paul said: 'Why should Charlotte steal a brooch that her father would willingly buy for her? A brooch she didn't want anyway because she immediately gave it to you.'

'Paul's only saying what everybody's going to say,' Avril inserted quickly, thinking it wise to remind them of her presence. The atmosphere between these two had her blowing on her fingers. It was the sort of situation she preferred to walk away from, but being trapped with them in a fast moving car prevented this.

'It's the truth,' persisted Eve.

'All right,' said Paul. 'So all this time presumably the party is going on, and I'm kicking my heels downstairs. Carry on.'

'Charlotte was upset, naturally, and she asked me to stay with her until she fell asleep. Only I fell asleep as well. Lilith came in and found me. She put on some clothes and drove me home.'

'What time was this?'

'Going on for four a.m.'

'What did she say to you when you told her about Charlotte's taking the brooch? Not a very pleasant thing to be told about one's stepdaughter.'

'Which is probably why I didn't tell her. I didn't feel I had the strength.'

'Didn't tell her? That sounds strange to me.'

Not half as strange as a new thought that was churning away in Eve's brain, making her prey to a fresh fear. If Charlotte and Lilith refused to corroborate her story, who would believe her? Cheryl could have given the brooch to her. She'd never tried to hide the fact that she had a soft spot for Cheryl, and it could be thought she was placing the blame on Charlotte to protect the other child. Even if Lilith admitted driving her home at four a.m. all it would prove was that she hadn't repulsed Paul and gone home with Tony. *And Lilith would not admit it.*

In going over in her mind what had taken place in the early hours of the morning, the something that had been bothering her stood out clearly. By concentrating very hard, she was able to step back through her own thoughts and re-enact the scene. She'd walked the few paces from Charlotte's bed and sank into the armchair, feeling its deep comfort enfold her. Charlotte's spread-out hair swam golden in the pool of light from the bedside lamp. Deeply distressed as she was by Charlotte's problem, she remembered feeling light-headed with happiness at the turn her relationship with Paul had taken. Having to curtail the surge of aching, hungry passion she felt for Paul, who was waiting for her downstairs, his eyes full of sweet threat, was unbearable agony. She willed Charlotte to hurry and fall asleep so that she could go to Paul. Go to him and let their passions interlock and overflow until this clamour in her heart was appeased. She'd shivered deliciously, wishing her eyelids didn't feel so heavy.

She must have slept. She jerked abruptly awake to the realisation she'd been dreaming of Paul. That he was holding her close and her fingers were curling into his hair. His name was on her parted lips. But the eyes she stared into flicked her with contempt, and they belonged to Lilith. The bedroom door was open and she could see the hatred in the other girl's face by the light straining in from the landing. *Because the bedside lamp was dark*, although it had been glowing softly when Eve fell asleep.

Someone — Lilith! — had popped in to see Charlotte before retiring, following a nightly custom perhaps of removing a book from slack fingers. As she turned off the bedside lamp, she couldn't have failed to see Eve asleep in the chair. But if she'd roused her then, it would still have been early enough for Eve to phone Paul and ask him to come back for her.

In letting her sleep on, Lilith had intended mischief. Having achieved this end more successfully than she could possibly have hoped, she wasn't going to speak out later. If Paul believed her, it had to be because he accepted her word as the implicit truth. No one had *seen* to tell Paul she'd been driven home in Lilith's dark, wantonly luxurious car at four o'clock in the morning.

Paul regarded her tense, shrinking figure. 'Would you say this is a likely spot to begin the search?'

She nodded. Her mouth was in the grip of freezing foreboding. 'If we find her . . . ?'

'Let's take one step at a time,' said Paul, reading her thoughts.

They got out of the car and observed the bare, harsh, rock-strewn landscape, full of dark and remote places that could conceal a poor sick child. Daylight only partially alleviated the essence of powerful forces boiling and swaying in the blown heather. Eve, who knew the moor better in reckless exhilaration than in dread, was well aware of these forces. 'Please,' was her impassioned cry, 'let the night not have left irrepairable ruin in its wake. Let us find Cheryl and let her be all right.'

Even though she looked up to the blue sky, she could not blank out the dark, uncontrollable fear.

9

Having decided it was best to split up, Paul, Avril and Eve shot off in different directions.

Eve stumbled over the rough ground, urgency and fear whipping her heels, calling Cheryl's name. But the wind-blown echo was sent back to her. Only just fifteen, she thought. A solemn, sensitive little girl with too much responsibility placed on too young shoulders too soon.

Obviously the two men Paul had been arguing with in his study were police officers. It wouldn't have been known that Cheryl had disappeared then, the phone call about that came later, so Paul had been angry because the police had gone to Cheryl's house and seen fit to question her on so little evidence. How unfair that because Cheryl came from the poorer family, she should automatically be suspected. Nobody thought to question Charlotte, who had been in the shop at the same time.

It was a blessing that it was summer, and not the depths of winter with snow-lost roads and sky and hills hunching together at the bitter mercy of the whipping, whirling, obliterating wind. Had the calendar said January instead of June there would have been no hope at all.

Eve's eyes ached from looking and she was filled with a terrible sadness that spilled down her cheeks. She saw a flicker of movement between boulder and scrub, and her heart sank to recognise the streak of running beige-flecked rust as Paul's jacket. She'd never thought to experience disappointment at sight of Paul, or wish he was someone else.

Paul's arms opened instinctively to Eve, and she went into them like a little girl. He remembered how he'd first mistaken her for a pupil and had promised not to snitch on her for being in the staff room. He remembered how they had laughed together when it finally clicked that she was a teacher. And he would never forget the touching dignity of her that had raised her on tiptoe, as if unconsciously striving for greater height, and sparkled her delicious hazel eyes. The eyes still sparkled, but tears replaced the laughter, and all the bubbling happiness in her was lost in misery and mounting fear for this bitterly ill-fated child. Paul momentarily put aside his own deepening concern and held her close, stroking back her dishevelled hair. 'It will be all right, Eve. We'll find her.'

She nodded, her emotions brimming, enjoying the strength of him and the scratchy comfort of his jacket. 'Somehow, I don't know . . . but I feel akin to Cheryl. She could be my child.'

'Hardly,' he teased roughly. 'When Cheryl was born you hadn't reached puberty yourself.' His hand moved down and gently he finger-traced the path of a tear. He coaxed: 'Come on, let us resume the search.'

Yes, of course they must look for Cheryl. But if only this moment could be given exclusively to them. It was as if their mutual fear for Cheryl's safety had pushed away all petty differences, the anxieties and jealousies and misunderstanding that are prevalent between couples who are strongly attracted to each other. This harmonising was the perfect togetherness Eve had divined in imagery. The whole world shut out and just the two of them in a wonder of intimate sharing and quiet content . . . with all the sweet, racing passion just a kiss away. A very different sort of kiss from the ones Paul had bestowed upon her innocent mouth. But the golden kiss that would open the door to an ardour which was still only a half-awakened possibility. The kiss that would liberate the child and spirit the woman into a tingling ecstasy, a heady euphoria more than fulfilling its sweet promise.

'Oh . . . oh Paul.' As her mouth stabbed his name into his chest, her throat was filled with the quickened beat of her heart.

'My dearest and most aptly named Eve,' he groaned, wondering if she knew she was tempting him beyond endurance.

His hair was thick and crisp in her fingers, exactly as she had known it would be. His mouth warm and savage as it devoured hers and poured sweet sensuous joy into her heart, causing it to melt back in her eyes and on her lips for him to see and taste. Never in her most delirious dreams had she imagined a kiss like this. It went on and on. In the grip of delight and rapture, she realised on some still functioning part of her stupored brain, that this was merely the preliminary to the apex of bliss man and woman could experience. It seemed climatical in itself. The ultimate. Even as she rhapsodised the moment in her mind, so they were hurtling towards the brink of catastrophe.

The moment hadn't been theirs to use for their own pleasure, but had been greedily stolen. Even as their lips clung, guilt feelings began to stir. They broke free of the impassioned embrace to gaze at each other in horror. For allowing personal desire to come before duty. Neither of them realised that *because* of the horror of the situation, the need to come together for comfort had been a natural reaction. Which, just as naturally had triggered off deeper feelings. That blame didn't come into it.

'Good heaven's girl! What are we thinking of?'

Eve looked up, away from the censure and remorse in his eyes, but there was nothing good about the heavens. A heavy fleece of clouds was obscuring the sun. Dark silver and purple thunderheads lividly banked the hills from where they heard the first grumble of thunder. Dry white lightning flicked the sky.

Eve sighed heavily. A summer storm was the last thing they needed. In a burdened, unhappy voice she said: 'We must find Cheryl before it starts to rain.' We *will* find Cheryl before it starts to rain. But the thought had no substance, no reassurance, and shame as well as fear dogged her heels.

Eve could not keep up with Paul's long stride and was not unhappy to see him go ahead. When he stopped and seemed to be looking down into a dip or a fault, her heart began to thump sickly in her throat. She *knew*, before Paul shouted at the top of his voice, 'She's here,' so that Avril could hear too if she was anywhere near.

Eve walked to the edge of the fault, the fear of what she would see subsiding, bringing her nerves under control by effort of will. Avril materialised on the other side of the yawning hole. Eve saw Avril's face was streaming. Tears of relief? Or grief?

The which depended on . . .

Paul had part levered and part scrambled down to that bundle of tender pink. He bent over the inert body, lifted his face. 'She's alive. Knocked out, I think, and she might have twisted her ankle when she fell down here. But, thank God — ' said with the utmost and most sincere reverence — 'she's alive.'

He came up with Cheryl snuggled deep in his jacket. They walked to the car in uncommunicative grimness. As they drove to the hospital, all but the unconscious occupant of the car was hung up with a guilt that only Cheryl's complete recovery could expiate. Yet Eve and Paul's dalliance had lasted less than a hand-count of minutes. Both felt deeply shocked at letting the dangerous undertow of desire drag them from the search for even a second. Avril spent the time fruitlessly remonstrating with herself for pointing the finger at Cheryl.

Odd, therefore, to be warmly con-gratulated on the speed of their discovery. And to be told, on arrival at the hospital, that their quick action would undoubtedly tip the scales in favour of Cheryl's complete recovery.

'Will she really be all right?' a distraught, hardly-daring-to-believe, so repentant Eve asked the doctor in charge.

'Yes, thanks to you three. I wouldn't have given much for her chances if she'd been left out in this deluge for any length of time.' It was raining quite heavily now.

The rain beat down on Eve's face as she walked between Avril and Paul out of the hospital to Paul's car. It felt sweet on her cheeks. Cheryl was going to be all right and that — surely? — was all that mattered. But there was a sorrowing corner in Eve's rejoicing heart. The grief of the moment that had drawn her and Paul together for comfort, now dropped a constraint between them, wedging them even further apart.

Paul stopped the car at Avril's shop

for her to get out. With Avril's presence removed, the silence deepened. Could silence have depths? she asked herself. Yes, and colours. Golden silence, that sense of content between two people who don't have to talk. Black, bitter silence, between two people who, suddenly, have nothing to talk about.

'I suppose you are still seeing Adamson this evening?' Paul said eventually.

'Of course,' said Eve, feeling challenged. In truth she was dropping with dismay, because until Paul so bleakly reminded her, she'd forgotten making that date with Tony. Yet as far as Paul was concerned it was her life and she could go out with whom she pleased, as often as she pleased. The angle of her chin tilted to her thoughts.

'I only asked because I've a staff meeting to fix. I'd toyed with the idea of holding it this evening, but tomorrow will do as easily.'

So the query had been on an impersonal level? The indifference of his tone said that *personally* he didn't care. But after that kiss on the moor, he should care. There had been nothing impersonal and indifferent about that kiss. It had blatantly claimed her as his woman, not just for the given moment, but for all time. She was a one-man woman and he was the man who had sole rights of her lips, her heart, her body by right of love. It was inexcusable and quite unforgiveable of him to think she could respond so freely to any man but her heart's keeper. At this moment he should be telling her she wasn't going out with Tony, or any other man for that matter, because he said so and as far as she was concerned what he said went. Such was her longing for his unconditional mastery.

Paul came to her classroom late that afternoon to tell her that he'd been on the telephone to the hospital and that Cheryl was now conscious. She was still very poorly.

The bell rang for hometime while he was speaking. Eve waited until her class had dispersed, and then she said formally: 'Thank you for coming to tell me. Paul — ' She glanced down at her nervously twisting fingers — 'You do believe that I didn't go off with Tony last night, don't you? I was telling you the truth when I said that Charlotte nailed me, and that I fell asleep and wasn't discovered until going on for four by Lilith, and that she ran me home.'

'Yes. I believe you.'

'You do?' she gasped in incredulous wonder, her eyes and mouth rounding in delight. 'Despite the fact that I haven't a witness in the world to stand up for me, you believe what I say to be the truth?'

His hesitation was fractional. And if he chose to let his glance slide to a point above her head rather than allow it to be ensnared by the shining, putting-him-to-shame honesty in her eyes, she in her delirium was beyond noticing. 'I believe you.'

'Paul,' she said shooting joyfully into

his arms, twining hers round his neck and hugging him.

He was on the point of bending his head to her upturned mouth when it withdrew from its kissable state into prune-round disbelief. 'Oh! I'm so sorry . . . What could I have been thinking of?' Her breath bucketed into her throat and her cheeks began to turn an interesting shade of red.

He hung on to her, just in case she decided to go the whole hog and stop cuddling him. Happily, this didn't occur to her and he was magnetised enough to admit: 'Whatever you were thinking of, I heartily approve. Don't apologise for it. On the contrary, please keep thinking it.' As he spoke his mouth kept coming down until it met an acceptable, and accepting, softness.

In view of this warmer climate, he didn't see any joy in telling Eve that his acceptance of her word wasn't the blind belief she thought it to be, but that corroborative information had come from a very unlikely source. One Alice

Meakin who had pained to tell him of the disgraceful conduct of one Eve Masters, who had been delivered home by car at four a.m. that morning.

'It's not my nature to carry titbits of malicious gossip about members of the staff, but in view of Eve's moral responsibility to the pupils, I feel I should be failing in my duty if I did not bring this most unsavoury incident to your notice. I do not see how a teacher with such a frivolous sense of right can uphold moral dignity in class.'

Alice Meakin had flushed redder and redder, and Paul's mouth had grown tighter and tighter.

'The girl obviously isn't fit to be in charge of impressionable and innocent pupils.'

Innocent my foot! Some of them could teach Eve a thing or two. Paul had seethed inwardly, while finding infinite pleasure in thinking of her as a frustrated old spinster. Looking at her he wondered that this could be the same sweet person Hubert Rowland spoke of with such awed reverence.

'I thought you ought to know, Mr Smalley,' she said in a tight, sneering, prudish voice. A sound he could quickly have knocked back in her teeth if he'd been monster enough to acquaint her with something he thought she ought to know.

'What do you suggest I do?' he said in freezing sarcasm. 'Instant dismissal, do you think?'

Alice Meakin paled visably. 'Oh . . . I don't think . . . That sounds very extreme. Miss Masters' dismissal would distress me most severely, and even though it would be justifiable action, it would cause me to regret mentioning it.'

By supreme effort of will, Paul had said, and it must be added that he was aided by the truth: 'Don't regret anything, Miss Meakin. I am extremely grateful to you for mentioning it. Er . . . hem . . . what . . . that is, could you give me a brief description of the car?'

Miss Meakin could. And did. And brief as the description was, a dark in colour, rather big and expensive looking model fitted Lilith's dark maroon E-Type Jaguar a darn sight better than it did Tony's white mini.

'Well, Miss Meakin. As you don't counsel dismissal, what form of action do you suggest I take? You do agree that Miss Masters cannot go unreprimanded for her lapse?'

'No, of course not. That would never do. Perhaps you could . . . er . . . come to grips with the situation.'

'Ah yes! I'll do that, Miss Meakin. I promise.'

★ ★ ★

'What are you grinning at?' said Eve, pulling away.

His eyes were pure sauce. Obviously he was enjoying some quite delicious joke. But although she coaxed, pleaded and pouted by turn as she begged him to share whatever it was that was

226

tickling his fancy, all she got out of
the infuriating man was:

'Would you say this is coming to
grips with the situation?' as he pulled
her firmly back into his arms.

'Er . . . I suppose,' she said, thoroughly
mystified.

'That's what I think,' he said.

★ ★ ★

Clarissa Masters was at the kitchen sink
when Eve came in at the back door.

Eve automatically screwed the top
on the decoratively twisted paprika
jar which her mother had used and
left off.

'What time do we eat?'

'Why? Especially hungry or going
out?'

'Both.'

'Staff meeting?'

'No.'

'Social then?' said Clarissa Masters,
trying to work that one out. Eve's air
of despondency didn't fit.

'Yes.'

'Why don't you ask Shelley Anne to go along with you? She's looking down in the mouth.'

'As I feel now, Shelley Anne can go in my place.' She wasn't in the least looking forward to her date with Tony.

'Many a true word . . . ' said Clarissa Masters, sowing the seed. 'Why don't you go up and have a nice cousinly chat with Shelley Anne?'

'You think I've been a bit negligent in that quarter, don't you?'

'Well . . . '

''nuff said. I'll take my repentant self up to make amends.'

'You're a good girl, Eve.' To Eve's surprise her mother came over and kissed her.

'What's that for?'

'Does it have to be for anything?'

'No.' But should that have been a yes?

Eve tapped on her own door, which was now Shelley Anne's door and yes, despite her good intentions, it still rankled that she'd had to give up her little domain.

'Come in.' Followed by: 'Oh, hello there,' as Eve's head poked round the door. 'To what do I owe this pleasure?'

'Now don't you get at me,' said Eve. 'I've already had that.'

'Really! Dear Aunt Clarissa. Nobody's ever wrapped me in cotton wool before and it's rather a pleasant experience. Have you come to tell me that supper's ready? The most delicious smell keeps wafting up.'

'It's goulash. I suppose Mum'll give us a shout when it's ready.'

'Ah! So it's talkie-talkie time.'

'Not for long, I'm afraid. I'm going out.'

'Lucky you.'

'Yes well . . . I don't really feel like glamming up, and I wondered . . . '

'Yes?'

' . . . if you'd care to substitute?'

'Would I! You don't know what

it would mean to go out with a reasonable, nice man.'

'What type do you usually go out with then?'

'The rodent variety.'

'Haven't you got over him yet?' Eve found herself enquiring sympathetically.

'Got over whom?' said Shelley Anne, her narrowed eyes glittering dangerously.

'The man you hoped to forget,' Eve said, barely pausing to bite the tip of her reckless tongue. 'You did come here to forget a man, didn't you?'

'Is that the impression I gave you? It's not the truth. I came, so that he wouldn't forget me.' Shelley Anne did not add, only it hasn't worked out like that.

Eve didn't need to be told that unwittingly she'd put her finger in a hornet's nest; she wanted to withdraw it, but didn't know how. Shelley Anne was looking at her in such a strange way. With her black hair and black glittering eyes and the skin drawn tightly over the twin spots of colour on her high cheekbones, she looked as magnificent and as regally beautiful, and as angry as all the wicked queens of fairy-tale and legend rolled into one. And Eve knew she had been right to be wary of Shelley Anne and regard her as a usurper, although the similar sounding word serpent came to mind, and the fear writhed inside her, ready to emit the poison of past grievances that were too readily remembered . . . too painful to forget.

'You superior, smug little prig,' Shelley Anne said, and her fury was all the more terrifying because it was controlled. 'I despised you for letting me take your toys away from you when you were a child. And I'll despise you as an adult for letting me take your toys away from you, whatever those toys are. Your lovely room, or . . . ' She laughed harshly. 'Substitute for you! Do you think I'll ever substitute for you? You silly creature, don't you know I'll take over from you?'

Eve blinked stupidly. Shelley Anne

was welcome to take over Tony. But could you take over something that was already yours? The feeling that some deep and indissoluble bond already existed between Shelley Anne and Tony was not a new thought in Eve's mind, which was now taking her back to that supposedly first meeting between Shelley Anne and Tony at the railway station. Hadn't the instant rapport been too good to be true? Looking from one to the other, Eve had felt she was getting in at the tail end of a secretive smile. She had talked herself into believing it was because they were both sophisticated people that they could converse by a nod, a lift of an eyebrow or the merest flicker of an eyelash. She had been envious of the mystique that elevated them to a wavelength unknown to her which empowered them to exchange words she could not hear. But it wasn't that at all. They weren't strangers . . . they might even have travelled down together.

No wonder Shelley Anne had laughed

when Eve innocently speculated on how her cousin had got that vast amount of luggage on the train. Her remark that obviously another accommodating mug had obliged must have sounded hilarious. Because Tony had been there at the beginning of the journey to lend a hand, and she was the mug for only just realising this.

But why the pretence? For what purpose? Might as well ask why the sky is blue or the grass green, why mountains are higher than valleys, because in just the same fundamental way that these things are so, this game of pretending was an integral and indivisable part of Shelley Anne. Life was too tame when played straight. She had to find a way of adding zing. Shelley Anne's voice seemed to come tinkling at her round memory's corner. 'I know, you go one way and I'll go the other way and let's meet in the street and pretend we've never met before.'

'Why?' Eve remembered saying stolidly, because if she was imagination's daughter she was also logic's child. 'For fun, silly,' Shelley Anne had mocked. 'And you can look at me and tell me what your first impression is of me. I want to know the impact I make on a stranger.' Whereupon Eve had dully persisted: 'How can I do that, when I know it's only a game and I'm not a stranger meeting you for the first time? I know you're Shelley Anne Masters and you can cross your eyes to your nose and you like it when the boys chase you.' Shelley Anne had demonstrated the one feat, but repudiated the other. 'I like it better when the boys catch me.' And then tossing her black hair. 'Oh, Eve, how stupid you are. You aren't any fun at all. And it's not all a game, because you'll always go one way and I'll go the other and we'll always meet as strangers. Always, do you hear?' And in that Shelley Anne had been right, because the closer Eve got to Shelley Anne, the less she knew her. And she suspected that was always going to be the way of it. She would never know Shelley Anne. She could think she knew things about her, but she would never capture the quicksilver essence and reality of her.

Again, Eve's mind switched to Shelley Anne's first day here. That evening she and Paul had passed the house Tony had rented, and through the uncurtained window, by flickering firelight, they had seen Tony and . . . this girl. Eve remembered how the girl willow-bent to Tony in absolute submission and how, just by watching, she'd felt an hitherto unexperienced sensation rising inside that was a positive ache, a pain of wanting. By comparison with this reckless, giving spirit, Eve had felt as innocent and untouched as a babe. At her door Paul had framed his fingers to her face, and instead of tilting her chin she'd wanted him to lift the whole of her through the shackles that still bound, into the brave world this unknown girl inhabited. Not an unknown girl at all. But . . . Shelley Anne? Shelley Anne with her black hair spangled with rain, insisting she hadn't been out. Shelley Anne who had just returned from her assignation with Tony, revelling in this hint of the clandestine . . . or something more sinister?

'It was you that first night, you and Tony.'

'What are you talking about?' Shelley Anne drawled contemptuously.

'We saw you, me and Paul. We were passing Tony's house and we saw through the window. We saw Tony and this girl and . . . '

'You think that was me?' Shelley Anne shivered convulsively and wondered if this were the nadir of all misery. 'You honestly think that was me?' she screamed at Eve.

'But,' faltered Eve, 'when I came up with the cocoa for you, your hair was spangled with rain.'

'Which only tells you I had been out. It could have been me. You are right to have finally worked it out that I knew Tony before. I went to see Tony that night, but I didn't get beyond the uncurtained window. I saw what you saw. Tony and . . . this mystery girl.' The words seemed to force themselves through Shelley Anne's dead mouth. In her white, lifeless face only her eyes were alive, still living the hurt and humiliation.

Biting the inside of her cheek, Eve realised she preferred the mocking hauteur to this . . . this despair.

'If it will help to talk about it?' she invited gently.

'Nothing will help.'

Eve evinced a sigh of relief at being let off the hook, because she felt life-battered enough without sharing Shelley Anne's burden. So easy a get-out was assumption only, a wrong one as it turned out.

'It won't help, but I'll burst if I don't tell someone.' And with that it all came pouring out of Shelley Anne.

10

'I got to know Tony last time I was in Spain. My parents' restaurant was the favourite meeting place of the arty set Tony went around with. I knew that he was in some way committed to a Spanish girl called Maria, but it didn't stop me falling for him. It amused him to flirt with me, while holding Maria's hand. That's why I pretended not to know him at Hawsbury station. I counted on the hint of intrigue putting the something missing back into our relationship. And then again, it was my way of telling Tony that I wasn't clinging as such. But that I was there if he wanted me.'

'He didn't know you were on the train, then? I was beginning to think you'd travelled down together.'

'No, no. He was knocked sideways when he saw me. He'd said goodbye to me some days earlier, and that was it as far as he was concerned. But let me tell you about the trouble in Spain first. Maria was just one of the many girls who fell for his charm. But — like me — she grew to love him too much. Maria's father was reasonably prosperous, but he didn't have the wealth Tony dreamed of, and so the moment she began to cling, he told her it was over between them. Which is when Maria's father stepped in and had a go at taking it out of Tony's hide. The incident made the Spanish newspapers. It happened in our restaurant and a quick-eyed diner picked up his camera and crooked his finger at exactly the right moment. Maria's father was a man of some standing in the area. The picture showed him up in a good light and was promptly bought by the boot-licking editor of the local rag. And so, for a few pesetas, I have Tony getting his come-uppance, recorded for ever in black and white.'

So that was the dark secret of the

Spanish newspaper which Shelley Anne had been at such pains to hide.

'When my holiday came to an end, I was over the moon when Tony told me he also planned to return to London. He made a note of my address and looked me up as promised. I honestly thought we had a steady relationship going until the day he came to say goodbye, because he was moving to Hawsbury. I said it needn't end there because I'd relatives in the district who'd be delighted to put me up. He was quite brutal. He said what was the point of moving to new pastures and taking his own daisy with him. I . . . I debased myself completely. I pleaded with him, told him I loved him and couldn't live without him. He said I was mistaking love for desire, and that I only wanted to marry him to possess. I should have learned from Maria's mistake and covered my possessive instincts, but it's easy to be wise after the event. Since I've been here, I've had time to think things out.

Pick out bits Tony's said over a number of occasions and piece them together to make a pattern. I know Tony is here in Hawsbury for a specific reason. It's my opinion he's stalking somebody.'

'What do you mean?'

'I don't know, Eve. When he explained about coming to Hawsbury, he said that someone had made a lucky strike and he knew a way of getting a share of it for himself. Your guess is as good as mine. It could be anything from acquiring a rich father-in-law to a spot of blackmail. He wouldn't scruple about how the money had been come by in the first place, or what he had to do to get his hands on it. Don't suppose you know of a possible victim?'

'No,' Eve snapped quickly. She was thinking of Paul's strange affluence. Because the house he had taken her to view was beyond a schoolmaster's pay. But it sounded too underhand for Paul to be involved.

'I'd like to know who Tony is slicking himself up to meet at this

241

precise moment.'

Eve's heart lurched sideways. She said wretchedly: 'I can tell you that one. It's me.'

'You?' Shelley Anne's bruising glance made her feel a little sick. 'Well, well! Uncle William hasn't come into a vast amount of money. If he has, everybody's kept quiet about it. So who else do you know who might be of interest to Tony?'

Not exactly flattering, Eve thought.

'Isn't it about time you went to pretty yourself up?' Shelley Anne taunted.

'You said you'd go in my place.'

'That was before I knew your date was with Tony.' Shelley Anne's voice dropped to a whisper. 'I've finally got it through my head that Tony doesn't want me.'

'He must be blind. You've got a special sort of glitter that nobody can compete with and even outshines gold.' The truth, as she saw it, raced precipitantly from Eve's tongue.

Instead of having her kindness thrown

back in her face, as Eve half expected, Shelley Anne put her head down and cried.

★ ★ ★

The evening was not a success. Tony had planned to feed her; not knowing this, Eve had already eaten. The best she could do was keep him company with a glass of wine.

At Nick's and Lilith's party she'd found it easy to talk to Tony, but of course it hadn't been talk as such. They'd made party noises, and in that atmosphere had been easy with one another. Eve had a stab at talking about the party, thinking that at least would be a pleasant and innocuous topic, only to find she met with a strange resistance.

'You didn't tell me whose friend you were, Lilith's or Nick's.'

'No, I didn't,' he said, very deliberately.

'I'm sorry. I didn't mean to pry. I

was just making conversation.'

'Conversation should never be made. Manufactured patter is phoney.'

She agreed. On noticing the inflexible lines of his mouth she wouldn't have dared to disagree, even if she hadn't held the same view. For the first time she saw behind the superficial mask. Tony was not for laughs all through. Beneath the blandness ran a deeply incised streak of hardness, a sort of determined ruthlessness. The thought gave access to a finger-tug of fear.

'Lilith,' he said so abruptly that she jumped.

'Lilith what?'

'I'm acquainted with Lilith. Since you are so interested.'

Did he think she was questioning him along calculated lines, and not just speaking at random?

At last the evening came to a close. She hoped, somewhat forlornly, he wouldn't want to kiss her goodnight, knowing that Tony would not pay for a girl's wine without thoughts of reward.

'Here we are,' she said briskly, as he brought the car to a standstill outside her door. 'Goodnight and tha — '

'No.'

'No?'

'It's no good getting the pip, dear Eve, because I'm going to kiss you, if only to fill an appalling gap in your education. How are you going to know if the schoolteacher is the be-all and end-all if you've never tried anybody else for size? Don't look so horrified, girl. You might even enjoy it.'

Tony had researched this subject most thoroughly and his technique left her breathless. But she was not a kissing for fun sort of girl, and she was glad when his arms released her and she was able to make her escape from the car.

'Thanks for the chemistry lesson,' she said mischievously,' and for my evening out. Goodnight.'

She half expected somebody to be waiting to waylay her, Shelley Anne perhaps. But the house was in darkness. Eve hadn't realised the hands of the clock had scraped round to such a late hour. She went straight up to her room, undressed and brushed her hair. Then she sat on the edge of the bed, dangling her hairbrush reflectively against her knees.

She got into bed, thinking and fretting. According to Shelley Anne, Tony was not here to paint, but was stalking somebody. Could it be Paul? Paul had been openly antagonistic towards Tony at the party. She'd thought it was because Tony had been paying attention to her. But now, Eve couldn't help wondering if it might be because Paul feared . . . what? Was there something in Paul's past he preferred to keep secret? Not something black and criminal, but one of the grey shades of wrong. Should she warn Paul? Or was it just another of Shelley Anne's fantasies? She hoped this was the case. In the event she decided to say nothing to Paul, for the simple reason that she couldn't think of a tasteful way to introduce the subject.

* * *

Cheryl's name was removed from the hospital danger list. As head injuries are always suspect, everyone breathed a little easier. A remorseful Charlotte was given a stiff talking to, and the matter was considered closed.

* * *

Swinging out of the school gates at lunch time, a woman's gentle voice halted Eve.

'Excuse me, but are you Eve Masters?'

'Yes,' said Eve.

'You don't know me, but I've heard so much about you from my granddaughter that I had to stop and say hello. I'm staying with my daughter and her husband at the moment. Just a short holiday.'

'How nice,' Eve murmured agreeably, looking into a pale face that seemed vaguely familiar.

It was a longish face, with still beautiful eyes, clear and grey and rather deep set. Mysterious and alive eyes, and yet it was a tired face, with the lines of strain as deeply etched as the lines of laughter. As if life had constantly badgered and made her weary, but still she came up smiling. The faded blonde hair caught the sun, turning it into a mimosa ball as it was momentarily given back the gold it had known in its youth. This woman reminded Eve strongly of someone. She taught her granddaughter. But although Eve diligently searched her memory, she couldn't find a face in her class to fit the one standing before her now. Then it came. The blonde hair, the grey eyes. Lilith Brookes!

'I'm waiting for Charlotte, now,' confirmed the woman. She smiled. 'I see I have gained an unfair advantage by not stating my name. I'm Sophie Rowland. Lilith Brookes is my daughter.'

The full significance of the woman's identity did not strike Eve straight away. She said goodbye to Sophie Rowland. Thinking, as she walked away, how generous of her to refer to Charlotte Brookes as her granddaughter, as if she was related by blood and not her daughter's stepchild. Had Lilith taken this same kindly view, Charlotte would not have turned out to be a problem child, and Cheryl would not be in hospital.

And then the other aspect of it hit her. Sophie Rowland was the name of Hubert Rowland's estranged wife. If Sophie was Lilith's mother, then that would make Hubert Rowland Lilith's father. So that explained the funny looks and odd interchanges between Hubert Rowland and Paul when they'd all dined together. And was the reason Paul had urged Mr Rowland to go with them to Lilith's and Nick's, knowing he'd be welcome in his daughter's house. Also, hadn't Paul told her that Hubert Rowland wanted the house, to be near his daughter.

Something rather ironic occurred to Eve. That lunchtime when Alice Meakin caught a glimpse of her Bert, she confided in Eve and one other person, Hubert Rowland's daughter, Lilith Brookes. The child of the marriage Alice didn't know anything about. Ironic . . . and very sad.

Eve's mind went back to Sophie Rowland, the sweet wife Hubert Rowland had turned from. And for what? For a dream. Hubert Rowland was a darling man and she liked him immensely, but he did have a slightly salty tongue to match his robust personality. He wouldn't even like Alice Meakin as she was now. If ever they came face to face, she bet he'd scuttle back to his wife quick enough. No, Eve. Keep out. It's none of your business. You musn't interfere.

★ ★ ★

When school had finished for the day, Eve hung on the few extra minutes to walk home with Paul.

'Coming in for a quick cuppa?' she asked, as they slowed at her door.

'M'm, that would be nice,' Paul accepted.

Shelley Anne's distinctive perfume met them as they walked in.

'You'll be able to talk to my cousin while I do the necessary. Coffee all right?'

'Perfect,' said Paul, his glance reaching beyond Eve to where Shelley Anne's sparkling black eyes were slanting him a long, assessing look.

White teeth caught at a pretty mouth in a quickly smothered gasp of surprise. Then, with a joyous skip that should have looked childish, but which achieved the opposite net result, Shelley Anne twinkled across the distance to be introduced.

'Shelley Anne — Paul. Paul — Shelley

Anne,' said Eve tensely.

'How do you do, Paul,' Shelley Anne said sweetly.

'How do you do, Shelley Anne,' Paul responded.

His eyes brimmed with laughter and, Eve noted abysmally, the appreciation Shelley Anne drew as a matter of course, was not missing.

She slipped quietly into the kitchen to make the coffee. She carried a curious impression, nurtured by something she had seen, and did not understand, in that delighted gasp of surprise Shelley Anne had emitted. Puzzling what it meant was like trying to look through frosted glass. Out of the several shadowy stabs her mind made, one came up rather clearer than the rest. Shelley Anne had recognised Paul from somewhere.

This conviction, far from diminishing, grew stronger as the minutes marched off the china mantel clock. Eve sipped her coffee. Paul's face was tilted at an angle of absorbed interest as he listened to Shelley Anne, who was in sparkling conversational form. Eve didn't quite know how she worked this out, but she knew it was a one-sided recognition and that Paul had not met Shelley Anne before.

Had Paul been pointed out to Shelley Anne by someone? For what reason?

Uneasy thoughts stirred in Eve's mind. For a long time she had felt there was something about Paul, something in his past that was unknown to her. But, and the knowledge came to her with chilling certainty, not unknown to Shelley Anne.

* * *

Eve rubbed the tips of her fingers together in a small chafing movement. Paul had left some time ago. Eve had finally nerved herself to confront Shelley Anne.

'You know something about Paul which I don't. I think you should tell me.'

Shelley Anne drawled with expansive malice: 'Don't you also think your Paul might resent such blatant prying into his affairs?'

Not prying . . . that made her feel like a compulsive meddler, with none of her loyalty and caring.

'I have to know.'

'Haven't you overlooked one small thing? I don't have to tell you.'

'No. But you're going to, aren't you?'

'No.'

'In that case — '

'You wouldn't be threatening me?' Shelley Anne's eyes narrowed to sparkling slits.

'No, of course not. I was going to say, in that case there's nothing more to be said.'

'You give up very easily, don't you?'

There was more than contempt in Shelley Anne's tone, there was something curiously akin to despair. A dip into an emotion that Eve would not have associated with her cousin, who, unless this was a delusory joke, was eyeing her with sympathetic kindliness.

Shelley Anne was plagued by a sudden driving urge to take Eve by the shoulders and shake her until she got wised up to the fact that she had no business having such a large inferiority complex. Having once cast herself as mediocre, was she going to go through life relegating herself to the supporting role? Never the bright star shining boldly, but the minor one that was too timid and unsure of itself to do more than twinkle feebly.

And yet there was that in Eve, some quality that gets under the skin, which made it not much fun taking her for a ride. If she only had the sense to know that if she looked back, long enough and hard enough, those trusting hazel eyes would ensure her a fair deal week, every week that went by.

Shelley Anne's mind melted back over the years. Triumphing over Eve had been an obsession. When had it stopped being fun? How long ago now since it had started leaving a bitter back-taste? Shelley Anne swallowed round a large guilt lump in her throat. Conscious that Eve's upraised face was expressive of puzzled comprehension, she deliberately avoided tangling with those dangerous eyes.

Eve was aware of the strange changes taking place in Shelley Anne. Instead of being on the cutting edge of her glance, she sensed she was in the presence of someone who was kindly intentioned towards her. Better had it been an illusory metamorphosis. At worst, Shelley Anne was a tricky customer to deal with. Eve felt weaponless against the formidable prospect of this sweet best.

And yet, it didn't come as a surprise. The changeling story she had woven round Shelley Anne as a child, sprung effortlessly to mind. It had not seemed possible for someone of Shelley Anne's delicacy and beauty to be mortal. So she had arrived at the only satisfactory explanation, that Shelley Anne had been substituted at birth for an exquisite and quite perfect fairy child. Eve felt she had always known the fairies hadn't taken that other child away, and that all these years she'd hidden, defying detection, in this beautiful impostor, waiting to emerge one day when the time was right. Or was this another fairy-tale, sequel to the first; an extravagant indulgence on her part to hope that Shelley Anne could be the friend she'd always longed to find in her cousin?

Shelley Anne flung up her hands and shouted vehemently: 'Stop being so defensive and start asserting yourself. When are you going to learn that nobody pushes you into second place, you scoot there of your own accord. Will you take a piece of advice from someone who is a million years old? You might bear the name Eve, but I am the one who has inherited an ancient wisdom from the first woman. So I beg of you to reach out and take what you want in this world, because nobody's going to hand it to you.'

'I don't know why you are talking to me like this.'

'It's because you're such a sweet person. Just for once, I'd like to see you come out top.'

Eve's eyes filled with tears. 'I've always known there was another Shelley Anne inside. But I thought she'd be plain. I never suspected she'd be more beautiful still.'

'Fiddle. By the way, I'm leaving tomorrow.'

'So soon? Why didn't you say?'

'And let you gloat for days over having your room back! No, truthfully, I've only just decided. I bumped into Tony. He told me he was preparing to leave Hawsbury. So there's no point in my staying.'

'Do you mean you're following him?'

'No. That's all finished.'

'Have you got over him?'

'One doesn't get over Tony in a hurry. I've wrenched him out of my heart by the roots. But it's like a pulled tooth. Until the wound heals, it hurts even more than it did before.'

'Where will you go?'

'Back to London for a while. Then I might join up with my parents again. Who knows! I'll have to think about it.'

'Will you tell me what you know about Paul?'

'If you insist.'

And yet, for Eve's own good, it would be better to withhold the truth. Eve was likely to run away from him if she thought he was a catch; but she'd dig herself in at his side if she believed he was in some kind of trouble. A sly smile broke through the solemnity of Shelley Anne's features. This was more her element. To deviate from the truth was like falling back into a familiar dance routine.

'Your man is going to need a loving and loyal companion by his side.'

'You mean . . . ?' Eve went sickly pale.

'I mean that Paul Smalley is not what he seems.'

'I've changed my mind. I don't want to hear any more. Somehow you've found out Paul's secret. Don't betray him, please.'

'Not even to you?'

'It doesn't matter to me. Whatever he's done can't make a scrap of difference to the way I feel.'

Afterwards, frowning over the conversation in her mind, Shelley Anne realised that every word she had spoken had been the white shining truth. Paul was not what he seemed. What man was? And every man needed a loving and loyal companion by his side!

She shuddered in amusement as she lifted down her suitcase. Time she moved beyond the scope of Eve's influence. Telling the truth could become a habit!

Springing the locks and lifting back the lid of the first suitcase, her eyes fell on the Spanish newspaper, the one she had been careful not to let Eve see for no other reason than it carried a picture of Tony.

She would keep it, and perhaps when the pain of a love denied left her heart, she might derive amusement in seeing Tony being punched on the nose by the father of the Spanish girl he had so cruelly cast aside. At the time, and not to gloat, either, but motivated by sympathy, she had gone to Maria and said: 'I'm sorry. I know how you feel.' The tragic-eyed Spanish girl had replied prophetically: 'You don't. But you will one day, when Tony casts you aside. *La inglesa* will be advised to save her tears for that day, which will come, never fear.'

Well, that day was here, just as Maria had forecast, and more tears than she'd ever thought to spill filled her eyes and ran sorrowfully down her cheeks.

The print blurred. Shelley Anne pressed her fingers to her eyes to stem the bitter flow, and proceeded to fold the newspaper. But just before sliding it into its well-worn folds, she read the other item, immediately beneath, which had caught her interest sufficiently to make it linger in her mind. It told the story of a young Englishman who was fighting in Court to inherit the estate of his late grandfather, Pablo Alver. The will was being contested by the sons of the great painter's brothers. As in the English newspapers, he was unnamed, but the Spanish edition carried his likeness. Just a head and shoulder shot, and not at very close range, but studying it again, Shelley Anne knew that her surprised recognition on seeing Paul for the first time had well-founded roots. It was Paul Smalley's face that looked up at her from the newspaper.

11

To her surprise, Eve found herself fiercely missing her cousin. On saying goodbye, her parents had said how much they'd enjoyed having Shelley Anne to stay. But Eve had been the one to implore: 'Come back soon. And take care.'

'Why?' Shelley Anne had grinned wickedly. 'The devil takes care of his own.'

A remark which had made Eve shake her head. She knew how much Shelley Anne had been hurt. The two cousins had then exchanged parting kisses of true affection.

It was a relief when the school activities which had been taking up an unfair share of Paul's time, relaxed, and he became her devoted escort.

One evening, after a wonderful meal in a restaurant famed for its cuisine, and by this time Eve had stopped worrying whether or not he could afford it, Eve made a point of mentioning: 'Did I tell you I met Hubert Rowland's wife. She came up to me and introduced herself, one lunchtime, as I was leaving school.'

'And you're wondering how Hubert Rowland could prefer our Miss Meakin to Sophie Rowland?'

'Am I that transparant?' Eve gasped in mortification.

'M'm, not really. I just happened to have made an intensive study of the subject most dear to my heart.'

How sweet, thought Eve.

'I happen to know you better than most.' He reached forward to finger-caress her cheek. 'So you might as well tell me what else is bothering you.'

'Well . . . Lilith.'

'Because it didn't click that she's Hubert Rowland's daughter?'

'Not . . . exactly. I think I should tell you that Lilith told me you two were once very close.'

'But *I* told you that Nick and I both courted the same girl.'

'I thought that was just kid stuff.'

'So it was, Eve. It was all over a long time ago.'

'When she started going out with Nick?'

'Long before that. Lilith didn't throw me over for Nick, if that's what you're thinking. In between, somebody came along to give her a bad time. I never met him. I can't even recall being told his name. Hubert Rowland thinks she's seeing him again. And I'm very much afraid that he's right.'

'What makes you think that?'

'Because I've more than a vague suspicion I know who he is. I've seen them together. And so have you.'

Eve was pretty certain she hadn't. But as she was about to protest, Paul said: 'It was Lilith we saw that evening with Tony Adamson.'

'The lovers silhouetted at the window? Are you sure the girl was Lilith? Oh, this is dreadful. What about Nick?'

'Hasn't it occurred to you that it might be Nick's fault? If he thought less about making money and concentrated more on his private life, perhaps he'd keep his wife at home.'

'You're not interested in money, are you, Paul?'

'I wouldn't go as far as to say that. It's useful. I wouldn't make a god of it, though.'

'Am I being fair in thinking that Mr Rowland came into his money *after* Tony finished with his daughter?'

'You are. Like to know how he struck it rich?'

'If Mr Rowland won't mind my knowing.'

'On the contrary, he's proud of the story. He dug it out of the ground. Yes, honestly. He was working on a building site not far from where an archaeological excavation was taking place. His spade struck what he thought to be a dirty old tin plate, which turned out to be treasure trove. His find is now in the British Museum and, as is the usual procedure for this sort of thing, Hubert Rowland was awarded the amount of money which the treasure would have fetched if sold. He calls it his lucky strike.'

'A lucky strike! Those were Shelley Anne's very words. She told me that Tony had come to Hawsbury because someone had made a lucky strike and he knew a way of getting a share of it for himself.'

'Even if Shelley Anne is right, and Tony is hoping to persuade Lilith to leave Nick, there's nothing we can do about it, Eve.'

'I don't suppose there is. Do you think she married Nick on the rebound?'

'Probably. But there's more to it than that. Nick's been married before. He's wanting to settle down with Lilith as if they've been married for years. Lilith not unnaturally wants the flowers and the flattery which is her due as a new bride. If Nick isn't going to supply it, then . . . ' He gave an expressive shrug. 'When it comes to the crunch, I should imagine Lilith will have the head to see Tony for the fortune hunter he is.'

Something else wouldn't let Eve rest. 'Paul? At Nick's party, you seemed to think you'd met Tony somewhere before. And yet you've just said you've never seen this old boyfriend from Lilith's past. So if you have met Tony before, it must be in connection with something else.'

'Yes. The feeling of having seen his face somewhere still bothers me. It's going to rankle until I can remember. To go on to something else, I'm paying for Cheryl to have a good holiday. To make up for the mystery surrounding the brooch.'

To protect Charlotte, it had been given out that Avril had misplaced the brooch, temporarily, and that it had really been in her possession all the time. But in certain quarters this was not wholly believed.

★ ★ ★

Assuming the holiday plan was general knowledge, next day Eve mentioned to Alice Meakin what a generous gesture she thought it was.

Alice Meakin flushed with indignation and said: 'I think it is the most scandalous thing I've ever heard. Do you mean to tell me that Mr Smalley is sending that child on holiday?'

'I thought you knew, Miss Meakin.'

'In my day, people were punished for dishonesty, not rewarded.'

Drawing herself up to her full height, Eve said in a dangerously quiet voice: 'I cannot allow you to slander Cheryl's name. Cheryl did not take the brooch. She has been an unfortunate victim and is innocent of any — '

'Is that what you really believe?' Alice Meakin cut in scathingly.

'It's what I *know*. But even if Cheryl had been guilty, which she isn't, I'd still say bravo for what Paul is doing.'

'You're a fool. Cheryl Carter is not worth your concern.'

'She *is*.'

'Your judgement of people's characters leaves much to be desired.'

'Can you be so certain your judgement is superior? Aren't you, or those you love, ever in danger of making a mistake? And wouldn't you stand by them, offer a helping hand, if they did?'

Eve knew her anger was both disproportionate and unwise, but she was incensed by Alice Meakin's wrong verdict and low opinion of Cheryl.

'That question can never arise. I've always prided myself on my ability to assess a person's character. I've never been let down.'

'Could I tell you a thing or two.' The words spilled out in a feverish imprudence and, much as Eve longed to pull them back, were beyond recall.

'Exactly what are you suggesting?' Alice Meakin enquired icily.

'Nothing. I shouldn't have said that. Please forget I ever did. And now if you'll excuse me.'

'Where do you think you're going?'

'Where everybody else has already gone. Home. We'll be lucky if the caretaker hasn't locked us in.'

'You don't think I'll let you go? You're not moving a foot until you've explained yourself.'

Bitterly regretting her reckless tongue — how could she have made so careless, so cruel a slip? — she knew that Alice Meakin would grind away at her until she related the sad story. It came to Eve that Hubert Rowland's existing marriage was too dangerous a secret to be locked away for ever, and that Alice Meakin should be told. But not at this moment in time, and not by her. If Eve told her now it would seem as though she was scoring off her in temper. Hubert Rowland was the one, and he must be persuaded to come forward and explain everything.

Alice Meakin's thin fingers were binding Eve's wrist like a steel claw. Eve didn't realise how cruelly tight the grip was until it slackened.

'Bert . . . Is it him?' Faded blue

eyes floated above Eve's head, glazed over with shock and wonder. 'Am I dreaming? I thought I saw him walk past the window. If it wasn't him it was somebody just like him, talking to Mr Smalley.'

'Miss Meakin, *don't* . . . '

But Alice Meakin was already jerking open the door and striding down the corridor, calling for her Bert to wait for her, her plain features transfixed with joyous disbelief. Even a tidal wave would not have deterred her, and Eve wondered why she had tried, having previously arrived at the conclusion that this was the only way.

Eve followed, close as a shadow, eyes glued on the two men, Hubert Rowland and Paul.

Paul looked grim, his brow was screwed well down. Hubert Rowland's face was a mask of shock and concern.

'Ally,' he said, reverting to the pet name he'd used all those years ago. 'What are you doing here? It's long past your home time.'

'I stayed chatting. And lucky I did.'

'No, Ally, it isn't.' The determined gravity of his mouth halted her flight, which was all set to take her straight into his arms. 'The situation between us will have to wait, which shouldn't be too difficult seeing as it's waited all these years.'

'I don't understand why you've come. If not for me, Bert . . . ?'

'That would be a happier mission than the one I'm on. Tell them, Paul, b-because . . . ' His voice appeared to falter, and gave out altogether. The tears that choked his throat, distressed his eyes.

'Lilith's left Nick. Her mother tried to make her see some sense, failed, and so contacted Mr Rowland. Lilith's gone to Scotland . . . with . . . ' His eyes flicked to Hubert Rowland.

'You might as well tell them the lot.'

'She's gone with Tony Adamson. Nick doesn't know yet. Mr Rowland wants me to fetch her back before he finds out.'

'Why?' demanded Alice Meakin.

'Lilith flung out in a temper. Mr Rowland thinks she might have since calmed down and be willing to return with an uninvolved third party.'

'No . . . no. I mean why should this person's doings be Bert's concern?' She looked down her nose, as if this behaviour was quite predictable and she wondered why everybody was making such a fuss. The disapproving arrogance and righteous indignation of her tone scorched Hubert Rowland's cheeks and depressed his lips to a thin line.

Even though Lilith was no friend of Eve's, she felt her fingers curling up in anger. And yet in apportioning blame, she felt that in not telling Alice Meakin long ago, Hubert Rowland was not without fault. Whatever distress Alice Meakin's censorious and unbending attitude was causing, was going to be paid back in full measure.

'Steady, Miss Meakin,' Paul cautioned, the only one with enough voice to endeavour to turn what showed all the signs of developing into a nasty situation. 'Lilith is Mr Rowland's daughter. Sophie Rowland, Lilith's mother, is his wife.'

Alice Meakin's chin rode high and inflexible. An angry fire leapt behind the pale blue eyes. 'How could you marry someone else? When all these years I've kept myself free for you. But . . . what am I saying. It's not the same for a man, is it? And I had my parents to stop me from being too lonely. I suppose when you couldn't find me, you thought . . . '

'It's true I looked for you, Ally. For years I never stopped searching. But I'll have no more deception between us. I didn't marry for companionship.'

'You didn't marry for . . . ? What are you trying to tell me, Bert?'

'Don't you know? I was already married.'

'I don't believe you. You couldn't be,' she said in a tinny voice, 'you gave me your ring. You led me to believe . . . '

A hand fastened on Eve's wrist. She smiled weakly up at Paul and allowed herself to be led away on curiously jelly legs. She wept inside for Alice Meakin whose entrancing spectacle of yesterday, the bright shining star that had lit the dimness of the dreary years between, had been dashed to the ground. Her dreams lay in splinters at her feet. Such a heinous confession. Not only destroying a perfect memory, but sullying it with human failings, bruising her high moral code beyond credence.

Eve felt no less sorry for Hubert Rowland. His awesomely straight face conveyed an inner disintegration. The crumbling of an image that had robbed him and his sad-eyed wife of a second bite of the apple. The chance of making a happy life together. Years of living lost, thrown away for an illusion.

'He'll go back to his wife,' said Paul.

Eve conjured up that pale face with those still beautiful eyes, clear and grey, but with the glint of happiness restored. Funny, heart-breaking, to think that in his gentle Sophie, Hubert Rowland would find the happiness he'd been searching for all these years. Because she knew that Paul was right.

Eve came back from collecting her handbag and coat, to find Paul examining a scrap of paper.

'The name of the hotel Lilith's heading for in Scotland,' Paul explained.

'You're going after her, then?'

'No. The fact that she left her address means she wants to be fetched back. But not by me. I'm going to phone Nick.'

'But Mr Rowland said not to.'

'He's missed the point. Perhaps he's too close to Lilith to see what she's really aiming at. Nick is attending a rather important business convention in the Midlands. I think Lilith's making a last desperate bid to find out which is the most important to him. Her, or his business interests. Charlotte's not the only one who's found it necessary to cry out for help.'

Eve stayed outside his study while he telephoned.

On rejoining her, he said: 'It's up to Nick, now. I've a feeling it's time I put my own house in order. But not here. Let's go somewhere private where we can talk. My landlady's visiting her daughter in Harrogate. The most private place I can think of is her front parlour. If you can stand the flight of plaster ducks on the wall?'

★ ★ ★

Eve sat on the sofa in Mrs Taylor's front room. Paul remained standing, one hand lightly resting on the fireplace.

'About Tony Adamson. You know I'd got it in my head that I'd met him somewhere before? I was on the wrong track there. We'd never met. His face was familiar because I'd seen a picture of him in a newspaper. The same page

278

carried an item about me.'

'About you? It wasn't a Spanish newspaper, by any chance?' If it was the same newspaper Shelley Anne carried around with her, it would explain how she knew something about Paul.

'Well . . . yes.' He didn't frustrate her by asking her how she knew that, but went on to say, 'Tony Adamson was waiting for me when I got home last night. He had a little matter of blackmail on his mind.'

'Blackmail!' Of course, Tony would have a copy of the same newspaper, and whatever it was Shelley Anne knew about Paul, Tony would know too.

'It's obvious he wanted to squeeze some money out of me to finance his venture with Lilith. Enough and a bit over to pay expenses until he could get his hands on her father's money. It must have been particularly annoying for someone of Adamson's nature to have thrown up a girl because she had no money, only to find out events later turned her into a heiress.'

Shelley Anne said he'd got it in his mind to blackmail somebody or acquire himself a rich father-in-law. It's a bit cheeky of him to attempt both. Whatever he's got on you, you don't have to tell me if you don't want to. Because . . . ' Abandoning her inhibitions, she staked her bet in a breathless rush. 'It doesn't make any difference to the way I feel about you.' Short of saying 'I love you' she couldn't have made it much plainer. She screwed her eyes tightly shut, hoping that if he didn't love her, he wouldn't laugh at her declaration.

When she prized her eyelashes apart, she saw that his eyes were lost in soft amazement. He started to speak, but his voice was so gruff the words melted back into his throat and were difficult to hear.

'If I started to tell you now, and went on telling you every day for the rest of my life, there still wouldn't be enough time to tell you how sweet you are. There aren't words to express what it does to a guy to know his girl loves him no matter what he's done.'

He sank down next to her on the sofa. He drew her forward and tilted her chin back with his finger. Her mouth quivered, her eyes were brilliant with the tears she was trying desperately to contain.

'Oh, Paul. I'm so stupid. You're not capable of doing anything bad.'

He had chosen to move by stealth, but not because he had something shameful to hide. Her heart was quite eloquent on that fact.

'Thank you.' Said with a simplicity and gravity which she found deeply moving. He reached into his pocket and carefully unfolded a single sheet of newspaper. 'This is what Adamson confronted me with.'

As she had suspected, Eve had seen its replica before. It was a copy of the Spanish newspaper that Shelley Anne had kept because it showed Tony receiving a punch on the nose from Maria's father. It was the item below this which Paul was pointing out to her.

'You almost tippled it once. Remember? Only the English version didn't carry my picture.'

And then she was looking at the smudged, but instantly recognisable photograph of Paul. The caption underneath was in Spanish, but the name Pablo Alver spun out at her. She remembered reading the account in the English newspaper which had gone something along the lines of . . . A certain young man, who wishes to remain anonymous, is at last acknowledged as heir to his famous grandfather's estate, the artist and sculptor, Pablo Vicente Alverez, more popularly known as Pablo Alver.

'I asked you at the time if you were Pablo Alver's grandson,' said Eve, her eyes rounding in wonder. 'And you said — ' She paused, remembering what Paul had said.

'I told you the truth,' Paul reminded her unnecessarily, because the inner ear of memory was bringing his words back to her. 'Perhaps I am the grandson of Pablo Vicente Alverez, only I don't want it known. Yet because I cannot lie to you I am being deliberately evasive.'

She said helplessly: 'But how can Tony blackmail you because of this?'

He guessed, rightly, that I'd go to considerable lengths to avoid publicity. I told him that although I valued my privacy, I was not going to pay through the nose for it. I told him to go ahead and send this version to the English press.'

'Is that what he threatened? Do you think he will?'

'I don't know. I'm hoping I won't open my door one morning to a barrage of press photographers, but it's a risk I had to take.'

'Paul Vincent Smalley, called for his famous grandfather. Your middle name is Vincent, isn't it? It's one of those truths that's just too incredible to take in. Are you a lot richer because of this?'

'No. I'm considerably poorer. I won't shock you by telling you exactly how much it cost me in solicitors' fees and one thing and another to prove my case. If I hadn't had the means, I wouldn't have been able to do this thing for my grandmother. It mattered to her that the world knew she was legally married.'

'It's a formidable lot to grasp. I'm still confused. Are you telling me that instead of inheriting a fortune, it cost you one?'

'A fair proportion of one, yes. My grandfather was not acknowledged as being great in his lifetime, and his paintings barely gave him a living. The people who have benefited are those who bought his work at a modest fee, and now find themselves with something of considerable value on their hands. It's only since his death that his work has rocketed in price.'

'Yes . . . I remember something being said about that. But, surely you must have some of his paintings?'

'I have one, and my grandmother has three. All four will be mine one day. But no matter how much they appreciate in value, or how desperately hard up I find myself, I could never sell them. I feel they should be kept in the family to be handed down. I've also a few pencil sketches and dozens of rough preliminary drawings, which have survived destruction. They'd command a fair price if auctioned. But, there again, I'm sentimental enough to want to keep them for my children. You know that my parents are dead?'

'Yes, you told me.'

'My father did rather well in business. He had both luck and genius and — although this might sound strange to you — I hadn't a clue that he was a wealthy man until he died and it all came to me. He was a modest sort of bloke. You'd have liked him, Eve. To look at him you wouldn't have thought he'd two new pence to rub together.'

Like father like son, thought Eve, swallowing deeply. 'No, it doesn't sound strange to me. On the contrary, it has a decidedly familiar ring.'

Bunching her hair in his hands, he kissed her chastely on the forehead.

This is it, thought Eve. That beautiful, awesome and awe-inspiring moment I will remember all my life.

'Well, Eve, are you reconciled to loving my grandmother and putting up with all my idiosyncrasies? Will you marry me . . . my Eve?'

She tried to say that she wanted to marry him more than anything else in the world, but her throat was too full of joy to be able to deal with words quickly.

A croaky: 'Yes,' had to suffice. And then his arms were fast about her, and his lips were warm on hers. Her heart slid into that kiss, conveying its own message, better than words could.

Other titles in the
Linford Romance Library

SAVAGE PARADISE
Sheila Belshaw

For four years, Diana Hamilton had dreamed of returning to Luangwa Valley in Zambia. Now she was back — and, after a close encounter with a rhino — was receiving a lecture from a tall, khaki-clad man on the dangers of going into the bush alone!

PAST BETRAYALS
Giulia Gray

As soon as Jon realized that Julia had fallen in love with him, he broke off their relationship and returned to work in the Middle East. When Jon's best friend, Danny, proposed a marriage of friendship, Julia accepted. Then Jon returned and Julia discovered her love for him remained unchanged.

PRETTY MAIDS ALL IN A ROW
Rose Meadows

The six beautiful daughters of George III of England dreamt of handsome princes coming to claim them, but the King always found some excuse to reject proposals of marriage. This is the story of what befell the Princesses as they began to seek lovers at their father's court, leaving behind rumours of secret marriages and illegitimate children.

THE GOLDEN GIRL
Paula Lindsay

Sarah had everything — wealth, social background, great beauty and magnetic charm. Her heart was ruled by love and compassion for the less fortunate in life. Yet, when one man's happiness was at stake, she failed him — and herself.

A DREAM OF HER OWN
Barbara Best

A stranger gently kisses Sarah Danbury at her Betrothal Ball. Little does she realise that she is to meet this mysterious man again in very different circumstances.

HOSTAGE OF LOVE
Nara Lake

From the moment pretty Emma Tregear, the only child of a Van Diemen's Land magnate, met Philip Despard, she was desperately in love. Unfortunately, handsome Philip was a convict on parole.

THE ROAD TO BENDOUR
Joyce Eaglestone

Mary Mackenzie had lived a sheltered life on the family farm in Scotland. When she took a job in the city she was soon in a romantic maze from which only she could find the way out.

NEW BEGINNINGS
Ann Jennings

On the plane to his new job in a hospital in Turkey, Felix asked Harriet to put their engagement on hold, as Philippe Krir, the Director of Bodrum hospital, refused to hire 'attached' people. But, without an engagement ring, what possible excuse did Harriet have for holding Philippe at bay?

THE CAPTAIN'S LADY
Rachelle Edwards

1820: When Lianne Vernon becomes governess at Elswick Manor, she finds her young pupil is given to strange imaginings and that her employer, Captain Gideon Lang, is the most enigmatic man she has ever encountered. Soon Lianne begins to fear for her pupil's safety.

THE VAUGHAN PRIDE
Margaret Miles

As the new owner of Southwood Manor, Laura Vaughan discovers that she's even more poverty stricken than before. She also finds that her neighbour, the handsome Marius Kerr, is a little too close for comfort.

HONEY-POT
Mira Stables

Lovely, well-born, well-dowered, Russet Ingram drew all men to her. Yet here she was, a prisoner of the one man immune to her graces — accused of frivolously tampering with his young ward's romance!

DREAM OF LOVE
Helen McCabe

When there is a break-in at the art gallery she runs, Jade can't believe that Corin Bossinney is a trickster, or that she'd fallen for the oldest trick in the book . . .

FOR LOVE OF OLIVER
Diney Delancey

When Oliver Scott buys her family home, Carly retains the stable block from which she runs her riding school. But she soon discovers Oliver is not an easy neighbour to have. Then Carly is presented with a new challenge, one she must face for love of Oliver.

THE SECRET OF MONKS' HOUSE
Rachelle Edwards

Soon after her arrival at Monks' House, Lilith had been told that it was haunted by a monk, and she had laughed. Of greater interest was their neighbour, the mysterious Fabian Delamaye. Was he truly as debauched as rumour told, and what was the truth about his wife's death?

THE SPANISH HOUSE
Nancy John

Lynn couldn't help falling in love with the arrogant Brett Sackville. But Brett refused to believe that she felt nothing for his half-brother, Rafael. Lynn knew that the cruel game Brett made her play to protect Rafael's heart could end only by breaking hers.

PROUD SURGEON
Lynne Collins

Calder Savage, the new Senior Surgical Officer at St. Antony's Hospital, had really lived up to his name, venting a savage irony on anyone who fell foul of him. But when he gave Staff Nurse Honor Portland a lift home, she was surprised to find what an interesting man he was.

A PARTNER FOR PENNY
Pamela Forest

Penny had grown up with Christopher Lloyd and saw in him the older brother she'd never had. She was dismayed when he was arrogantly confident that she should not trust her new business colleague, Gerald Hart. She opposed Chris by setting out to win Gerald as a partner both in love and business.

SURGEON ASHORE
Ann Jennings

Luke Roderick, the new Consultant Surgeon for Accident and Emergency, couldn't understand why Staff Nurse Naomi Selbourne refused to apply for the vacant post of Sister. Naomi wasn't about to tell him that she moonlighted as a waitress in order to support her small nephew, Toby.

A MOONLIGHT MEETING
Peggy Gaddis

Megan seemed to have fallen under handsome Tom Fallon's spell, and she was no longer sure if she would be happy as Larry's wife. It was only in the aftermath of a terrible tragedy that she realized the true meaning of love.

THE STARLIT GARDEN
Patricia Hemstock

When interior designer Tansy Donaghue accepted a commission to restore Beechwood Manor in Devon, she was relieved to leave London and its memories of her broken romance with architect Robert Jarvis. But her dream of a peaceful break was shattered not only by Robert's unexpected visit, but also by the manipulative charms of the manor's owner, James Buchanan.

THE BECKONING DAWN
Georgina Ferrand

For twenty-five years Caroline has lived the life of a recluse, believing she is ugly because of a facial scar. After a successful operation, the handsome Anton Tessler comes into her life. However, Caroline soon learns that the kind of love she yearns for may never be hers.

THE WAY OF THE HEART
Rebecca Marsh

It was the scandal of the season when world-famous actress Andrea Lawrence stalked out of a Broadway hit to go home again. But she hadn't jeopardized her career for nothing. The beautiful star was onstage for the play of her life — a drama of double-dealing romance starring her sister's fiancé.

VIENNA MASQUERADE
Lorna McKenzie

In Austria, Kristal Hastings meets Rodolfo von Steinberg, the young cousin of Baron Gustav von Steinberg, who had been her grandmother's lover many years ago. An instant attraction flares between them — but how can Kristal give her love to Rudi when he is already promised to another . . . ?

HIDDEN LOVE
Margaret McDonagh

Until his marriage, Matt had seemed like an older brother to Teresa. Now, five years later, Matt's wife has tragically died and Teresa feels she must go and comfort him. But how much longer can she hold on to the secret that has been hers for all these years?

A MOST UNUSUAL MARRIAGE
Barbara Best

Practically penniless, Dorcas Wareham meets Suzette, who tells her that she had rashly married a Captain Jack Bickley on the eve of his leaving for the Boer War. She suggests that Dorcas takes her place, saying that Jack didn't expect to survive the war anyway. With some misgivings, Dorcas finally agrees. But Jack does return . . .

A TOUCH OF TENDERNESS
Juliet Gray

Ben knew just how to charm, how to captivate a woman — though he could not win a heart that was already in another man's keeping. But Clare was desperately anxious to protect him from a pain she knew too well herself.